PHILIP PULLMAN

THE GOLDEN COMPASS

Ada

English translation copyright © 2016 by Annie Eaton
Jacket art and interior illustrations copyright © 2015 by Gallimard Jeunesse

All rights reserved. Published in the United States by Alfred A. Knopf, an imprint of Random House Children's Books, a division of Penguin Random House LLC, New York. This graphic novel was originally published in French as *Les Royaumes du Nord 2* by Gallimard Jeunesse, Paris, in 2015. *Les Royaumes du Nord 2* copyright © 2015 by Gallimard Jeunesse. Adapted from the English-language work *The Golden Compass,* published by Alfred A. Knopf, an imprint of Random House Children's Books, New York, in 1996. *The Golden Compass* copyright © 1995 by Philip Pullman.

Knopf, Borzoi Books, and the colophon are registered trademarks of Penguin Random House LLC.

Visit us on the Web! randomhousekids.com

Educators and librarians, for a variety of teaching tools, visit us at RHTeachersLibrarians.com

Library of Congress Cataloging-in-Publication Data is available upon request.
ISBN 978-0-553-53512-9 (hc) — ISBN 978-0-553-53514-3 (lib. bdg.)
ISBN 978-0-553-53513-6 (pbk.) — ISBN 978-0-553-53515-0 (ebook)

MANUFACTURED IN CHINA
September 2016
10 9 8 7 6 5 4 3 2 1

First U.S. Edition

Rescued by the gyptians, Lyra is traveling north to find Lord Asriel and save her friend Roger. . . .

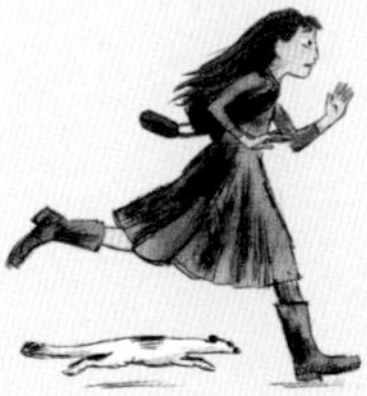

LYRA thought she was an orphan but recently learned that Mrs. Coulter and Lord Asriel are her true parents.

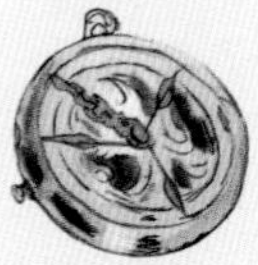

THE ALETHIOMETER, a rare instrument that allows the reader to find out the truth, was entrusted to Lyra by the Master of Jordan College.

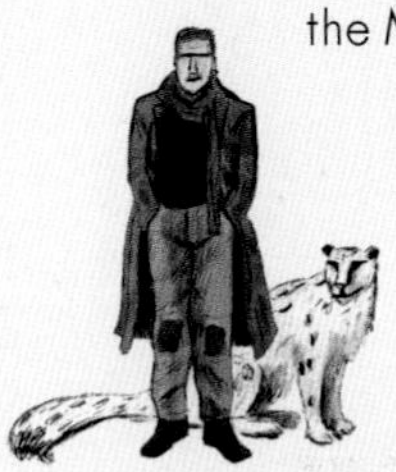

LORD ASRIEL, who is investigating the mysterious substance known as Dust, is being held prisoner by armored bears in remote Svalbard.

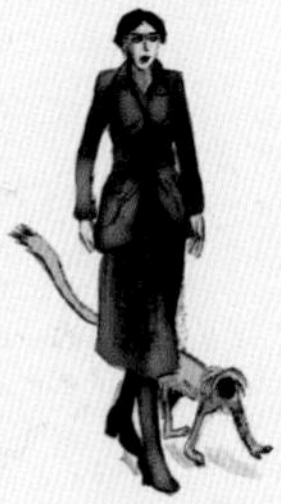

MRS. COULTER, head of the General Oblation Board, is probably behind the child-snatching Gobblers.

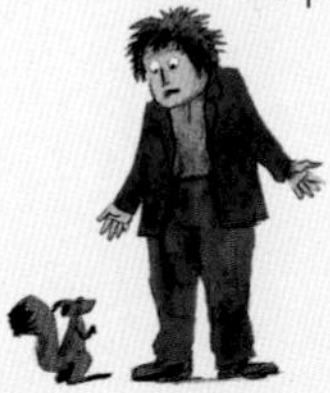

ROGER, Lyra's best friend, has been kidnapped by the Gobblers.

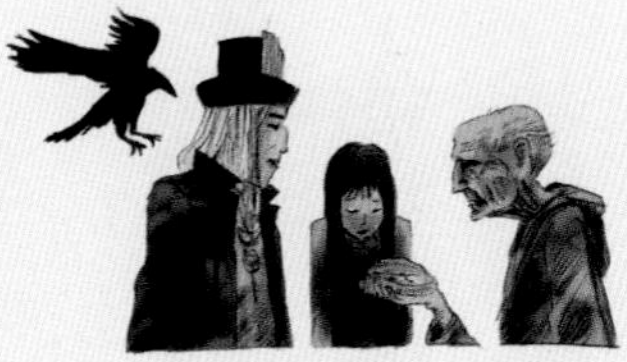

JOHN FAA, king of the gyptians, is leading an expedition north to rescue the children taken by the Gobblers. FARDER CORAM, the oldest of the gyptians, revealed to Lyra the identity of her parents. He once saved the life of a witch—whose help will prove invaluable.

For my father, Claude
—S.M.

Friendly wishes to F'murr, also to J.J. and Gégé, who, each in their own way,
have given me a love of wide snowy spaces
—C.O.

The word "dœmon," which appears throughout this book, is pronounced like "demon."

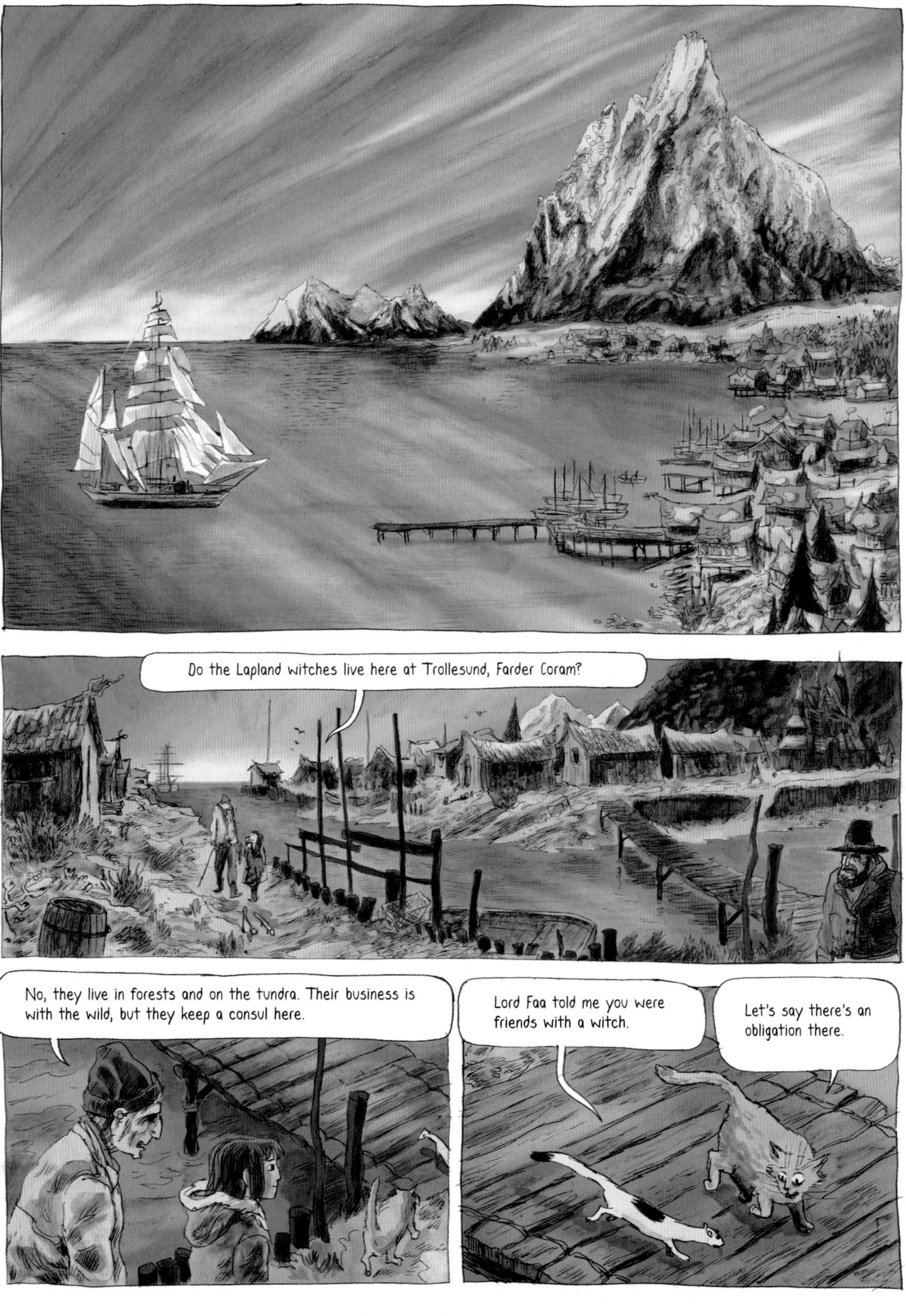
Do the Lapland witches live here at Trollesund, Farder Coram?
No, they live in forests and on the tundra. Their business is with the wild, but they keep a consul here.
Lord Faa told me you were friends with a witch.
Let's say there's an obligation there.

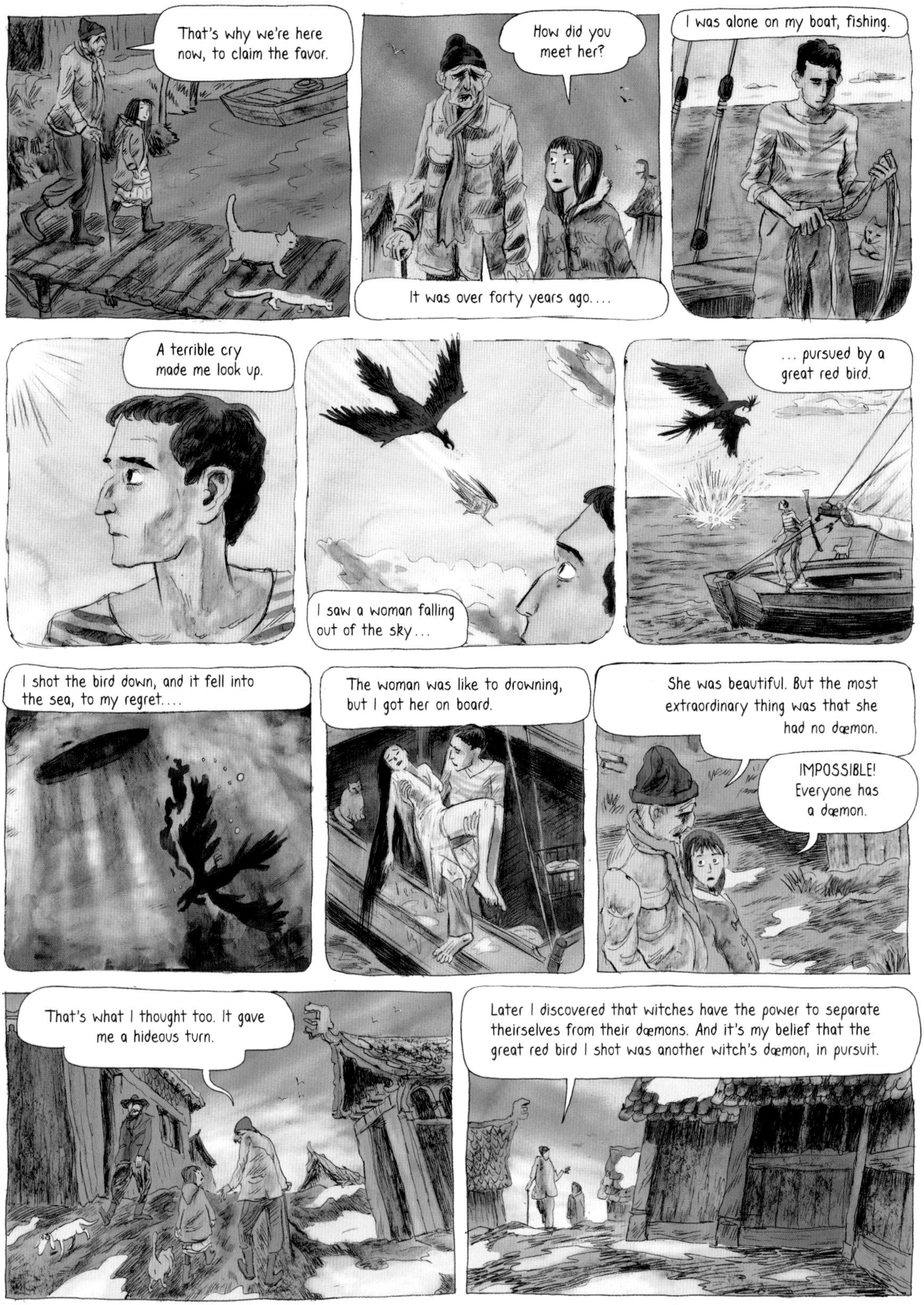
That's why we're here now, to claim the favor.
How did you meet her?
It was over forty years ago....
I was alone on my boat, fishing.
A terrible cry made me look up.
I saw a woman falling out of the sky...
... pursued by a great red bird.
I shot the bird down, and it fell into the sea, to my regret....
The woman was like to drowning, but I got her on board.
She was beautiful. But the most extraordinary thing was that she had no dæmon.
IMPOSSIBLE! Everyone has a dæmon.
That's what I thought too. It gave me a hideous turn.
Later I discovered that witches have the power to separate theirselves from their dæmons. And it's my belief that the great red bird I shot was another witch's dæmon, in pursuit.

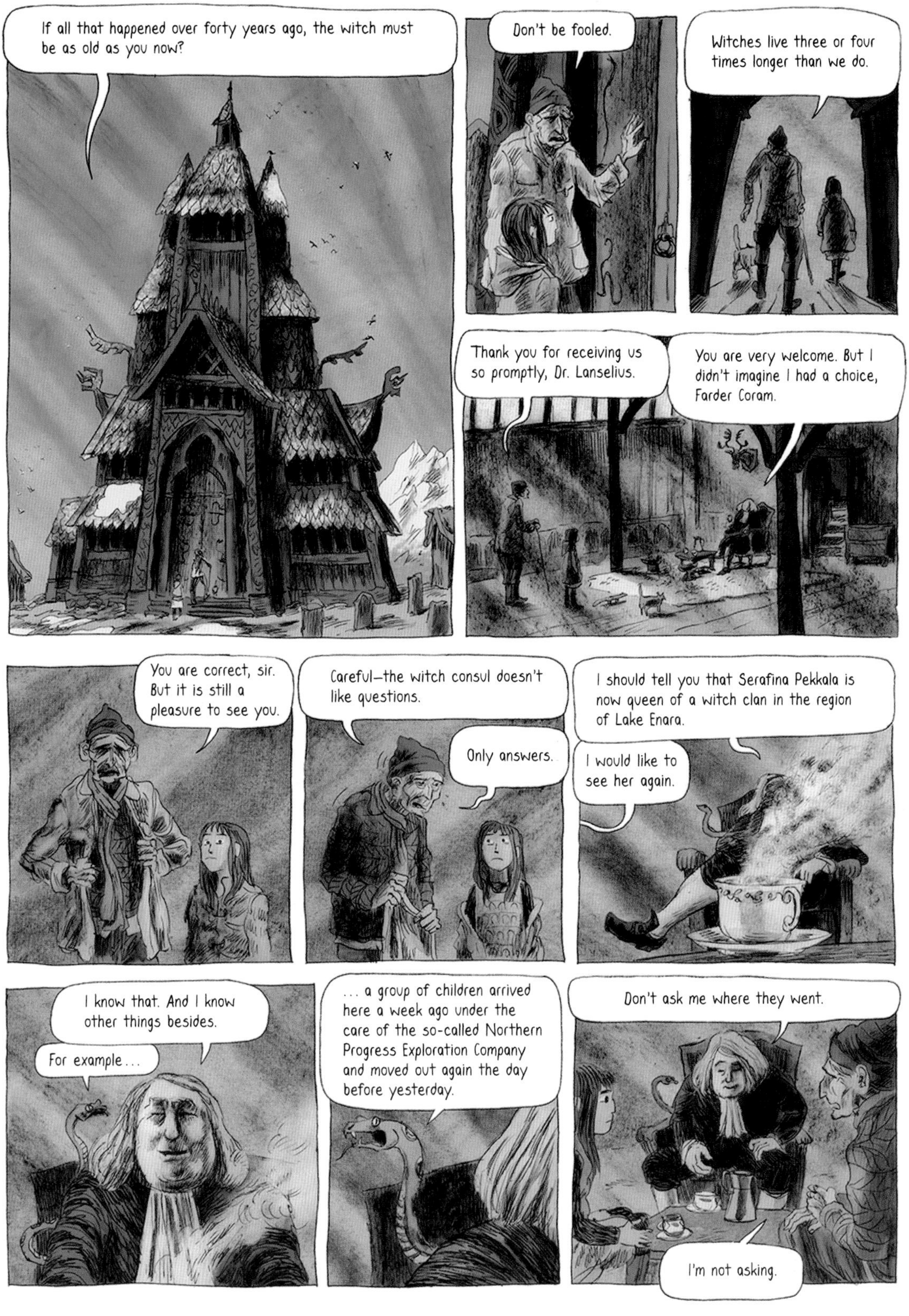
If all that happened over forty years ago, the witch must be as old as you now?
Don't be fooled.
Witches live three or four times longer than we do.
Thank you for receiving us so promptly, Dr. Lanselius.
You are very welcome. But I didn't imagine I had a choice, Farder Coram.
You are correct, sir. But it is still a pleasure to see you.
Careful—the witch consul doesn't like questions.
Only answers.
I should tell you that Serafina Pekkala is now queen of a witch clan in the region of Lake Enara.
I would like to see her again.
I know that. And I know other things besides.
For example . . .
. . . a group of children arrived here a week ago under the care of the so-called Northern Progress Exploration Company and moved out again the day before yesterday.
Don't ask me where they went.
I'm not asking.

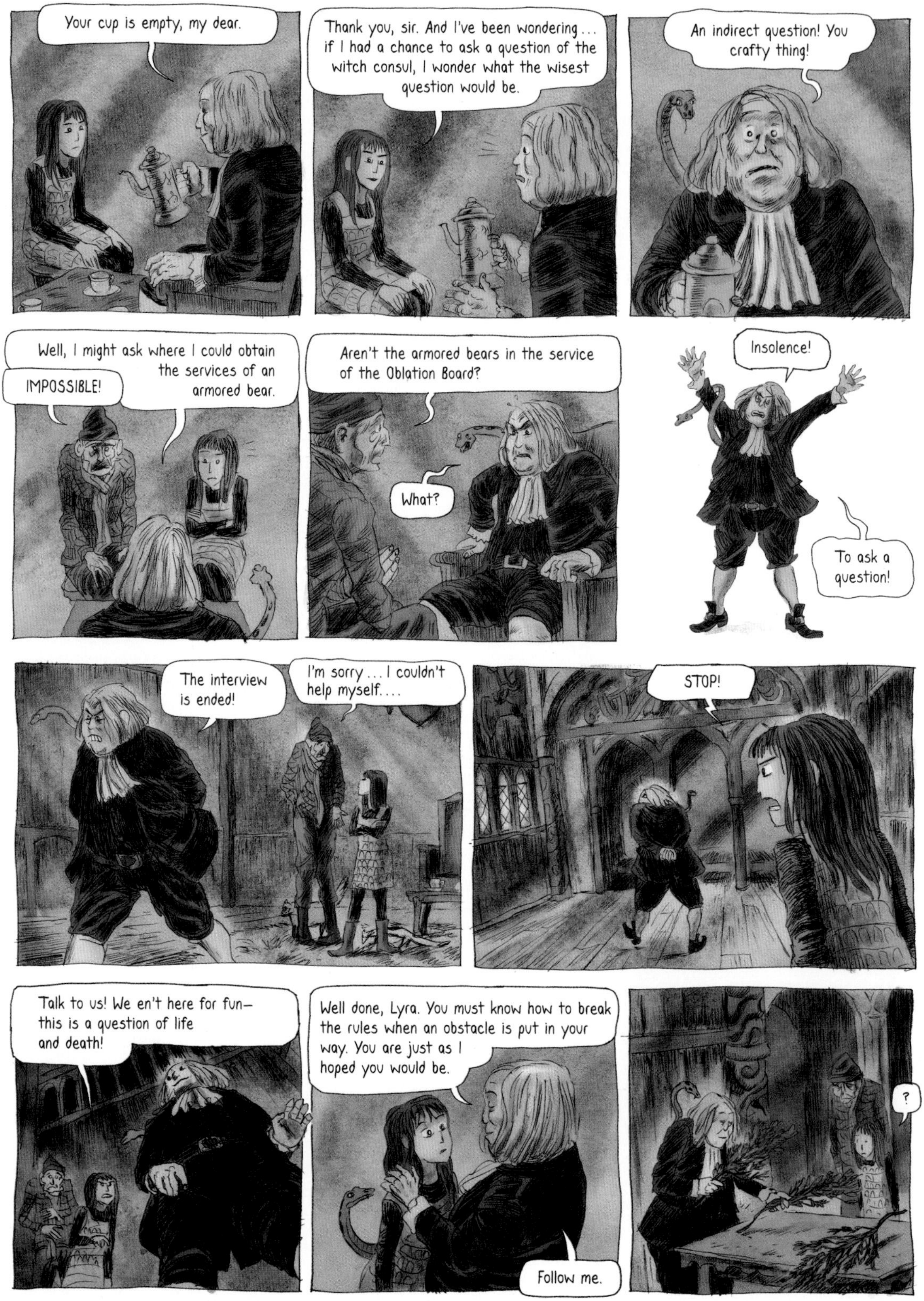
Your cup is empty, my dear.
Thank you, sir. And I've been wondering . . . if I had a chance to ask a question of the witch consul, I wonder what the wisest question would be.
An indirect question! You crafty thing!
Well, I might ask where I could obtain the services of an armored bear.
IMPOSSIBLE!
Aren't the armored bears in the service of the Oblation Board?
What?
Insolence!
To ask a question!
The interview is ended!
I'm sorry . . . I couldn't help myself. . . .
STOP!
Talk to us! We en't here for fun—this is a question of life and death!
Well done, Lyra. You must know how to break the rules when an obstacle is put in your way. You are just as I hoped you would be.
Follow me.
?

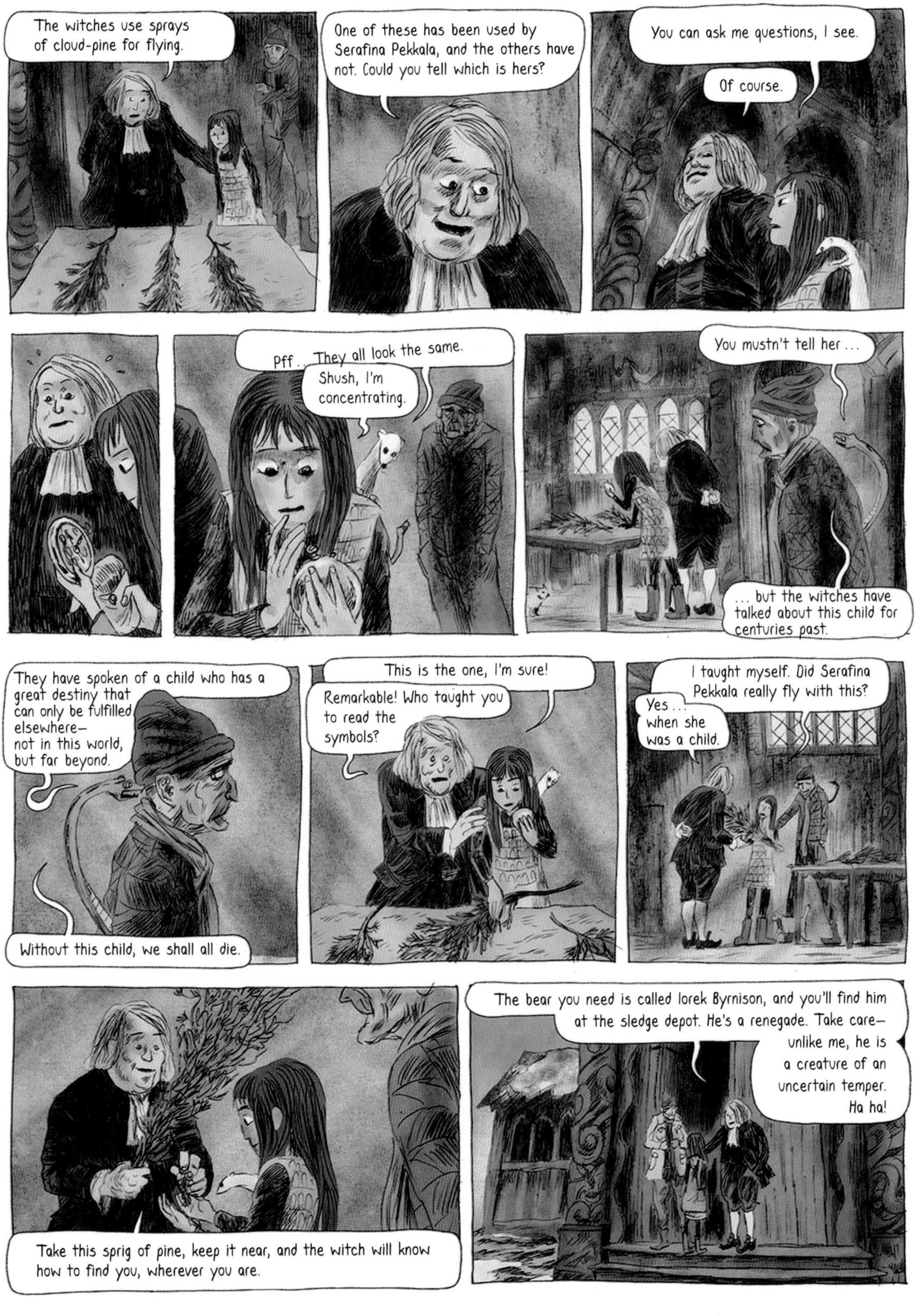

The witches use sprays of cloud-pine for flying.
One of these has been used by Serafina Pekkala, and the others have not. Could you tell which is hers?
You can ask me questions, I see.
Of course.
Pff... They all look the same.
Shush, I'm concentrating.
You mustn't tell her...
... but the witches have talked about this child for centuries past.
They have spoken of a child who has a great destiny that can only be fulfilled elsewhere— not in this world, but far beyond.
Without this child, we shall all die.
This is the one, I'm sure!
Remarkable! Who taught you to read the symbols?
I taught myself. Did Serafina Pekkala really fly with this?
Yes... when she was a child.
Take this sprig of pine, keep it near, and the witch will know how to find you, wherever you are.
The bear you need is called Iorek Byrnison, and you'll find him at the sledge depot. He's a renegade. Take care— unlike me, he is a creature of an uncertain temper.
Ha ha!

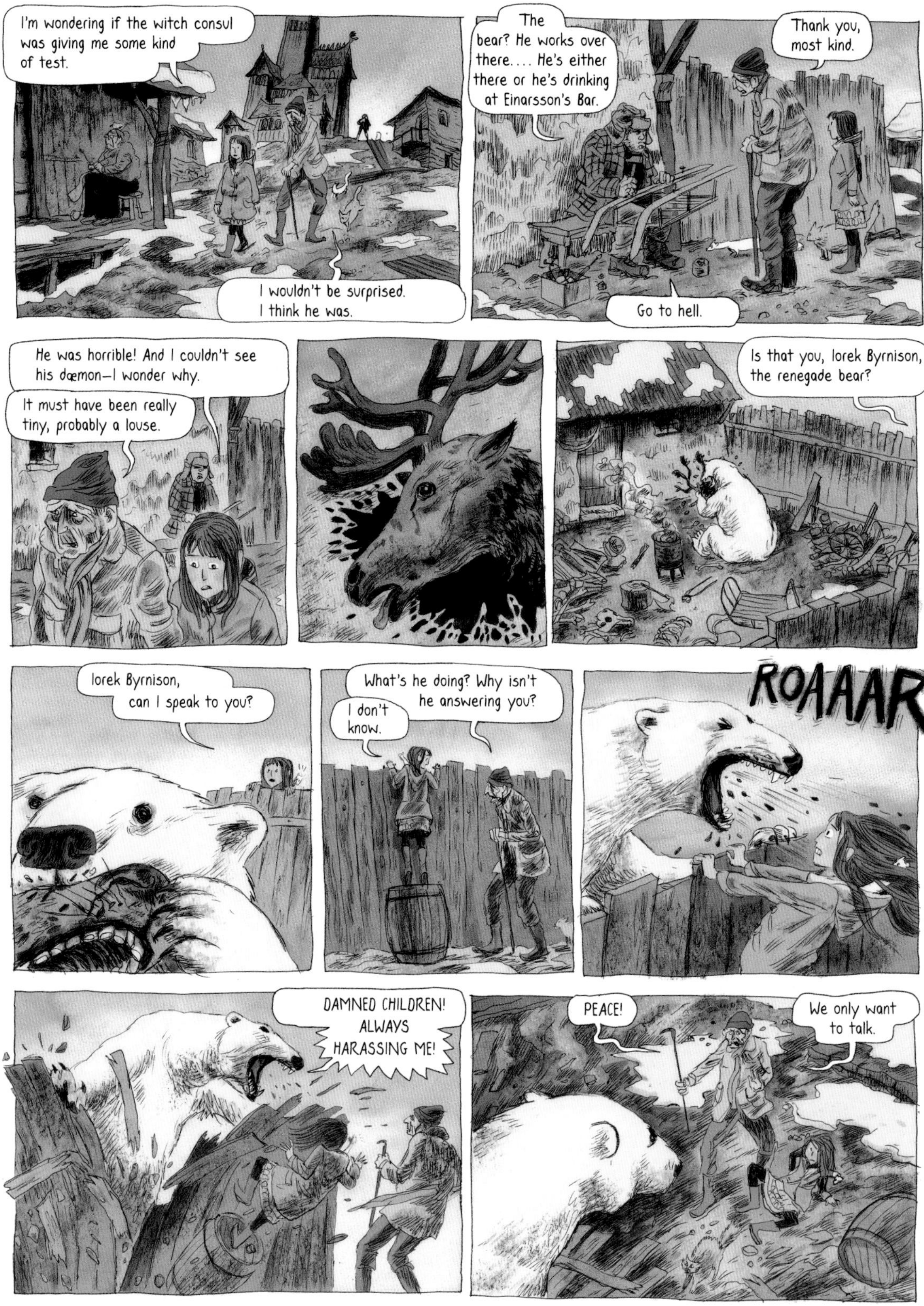
I'm wondering if the witch consul was giving me some kind of test.
I wouldn't be surprised. I think he was.
The bear? He works over there.... He's either there or he's drinking at Einarsson's Bar.
Thank you, most kind.
Go to hell.
He was horrible! And I couldn't see his dæmon—I wonder why.
It must have been really tiny, probably a louse.
Is that you, Iorek Byrnison, the renegade bear?
Iorek Byrnison, can I speak to you?
What's he doing? Why isn't he answering you?
I don't know.
ROAAAR
DAMNED CHILDREN! ALWAYS HARASSING ME!
PEACE!
We only want to talk.

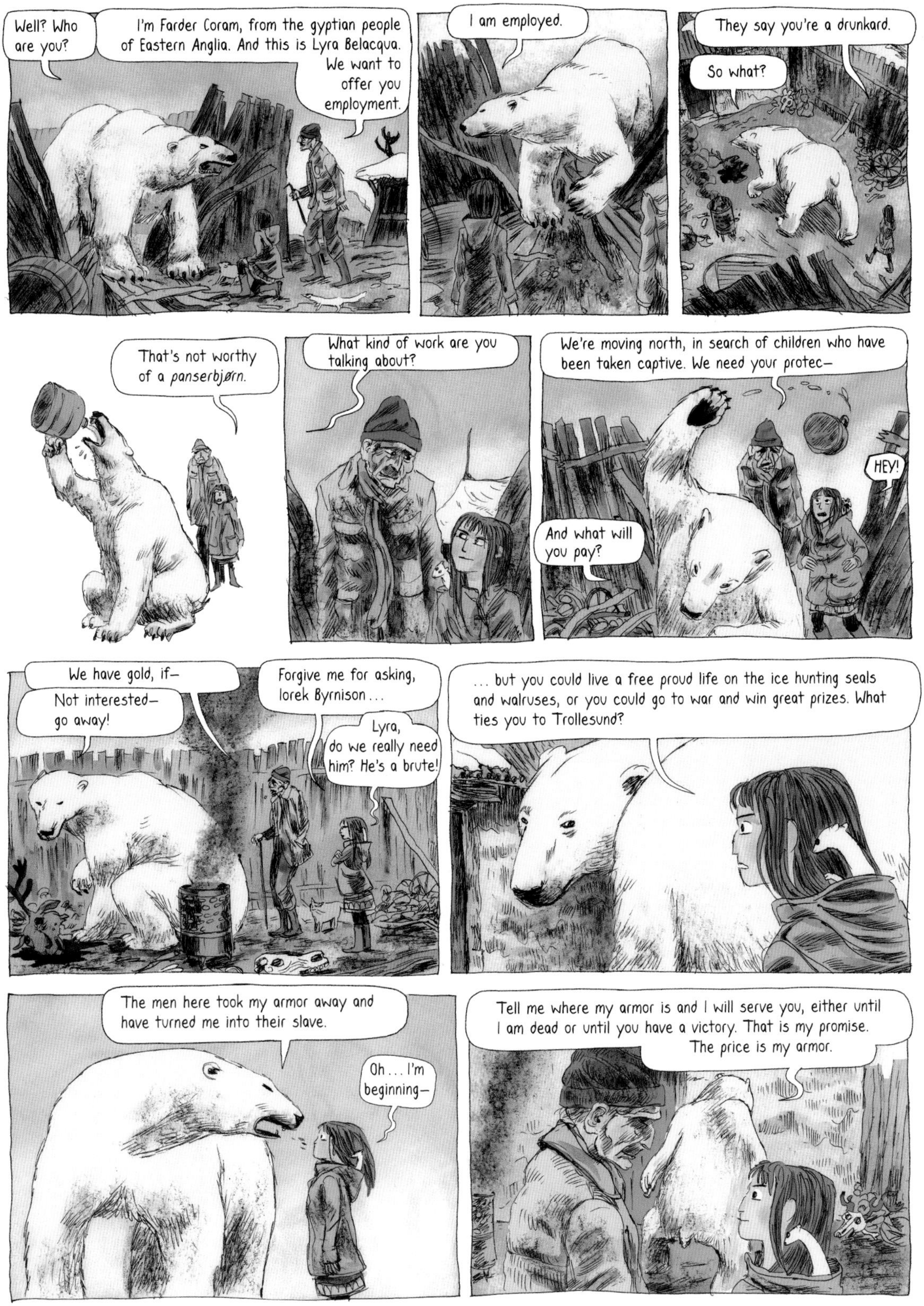
Well? Who are you?
I'm Farder Coram, from the gyptian people of Eastern Anglia. And this is Lyra Belacqua. We want to offer you employment.
I am employed.
They say you're a drunkard.
So what?
That's not worthy of a *panserbjørn*.
What kind of work are you talking about?
We're moving north, in search of children who have been taken captive. We need your protec—
HEY!
And what will you pay?
We have gold, if—
Not interested— go away!
Forgive me for asking, Iorek Byrnison . . .
Lyra, do we really need him? He's a brute!
. . . but you could live a free proud life on the ice hunting seals and walruses, or you could go to war and win great prizes. What ties you to Trollesund?
The men here took my armor away and have turned me into their slave.
Oh . . . I'm beginning—
Tell me where my armor is and I will serve you, either until I am dead or until you have a victory. That is my promise.
The price is my armor.

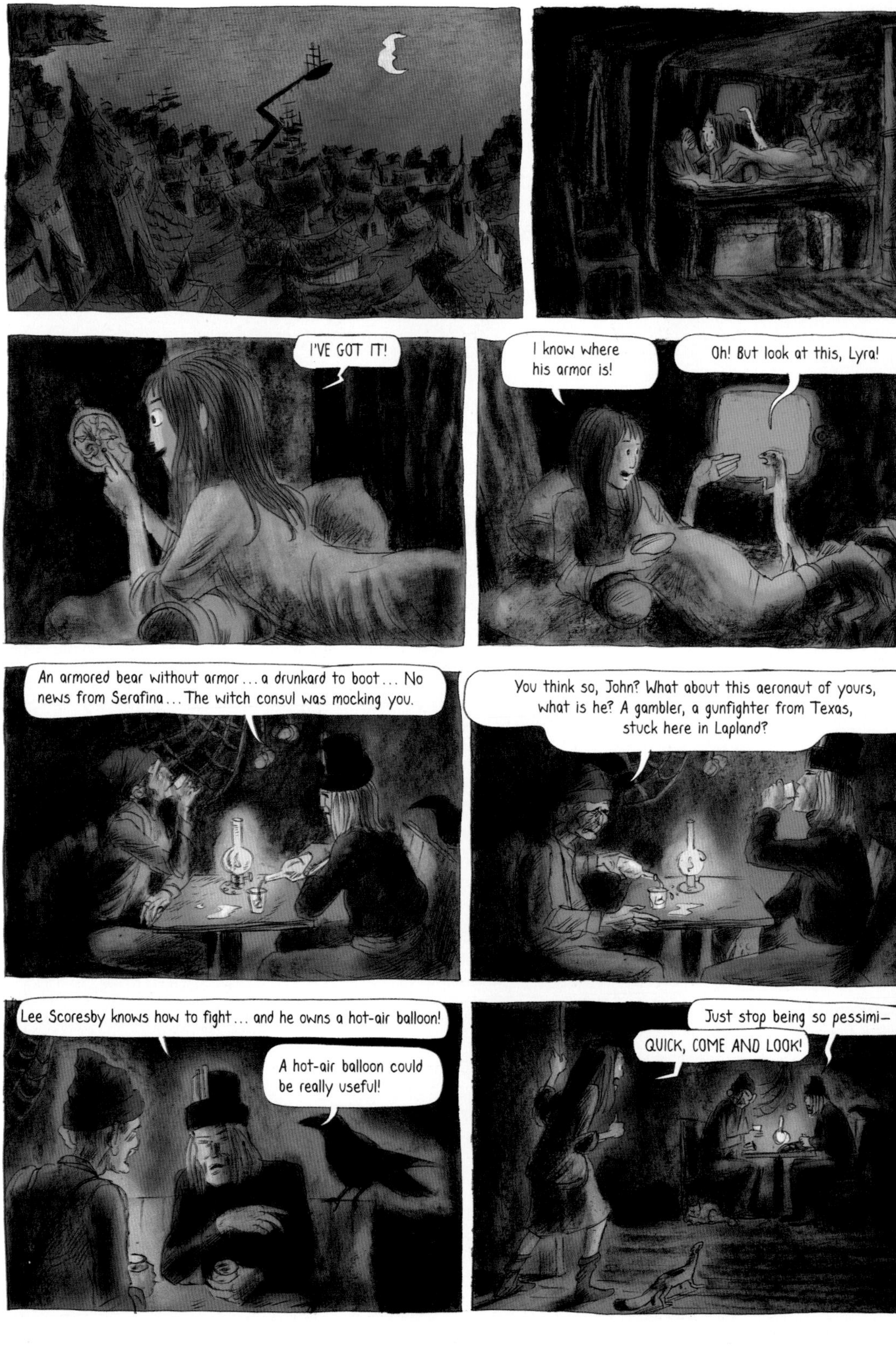
I'VE GOT IT!
I know where his armor is!
Oh! But look at this, Lyra!
An armored bear without armor . . . a drunkard to boot . . . No news from Serafina . . . The witch consul was mocking you.
You think so, John? What about this aeronaut of yours, what is he? A gambler, a gunfighter from Texas, stuck here in Lapland?
Lee Scoresby knows how to fight . . . and he owns a hot-air balloon!
A hot-air balloon could be really useful!
Just stop being so pessimi—
QUICK, COME AND LOOK!

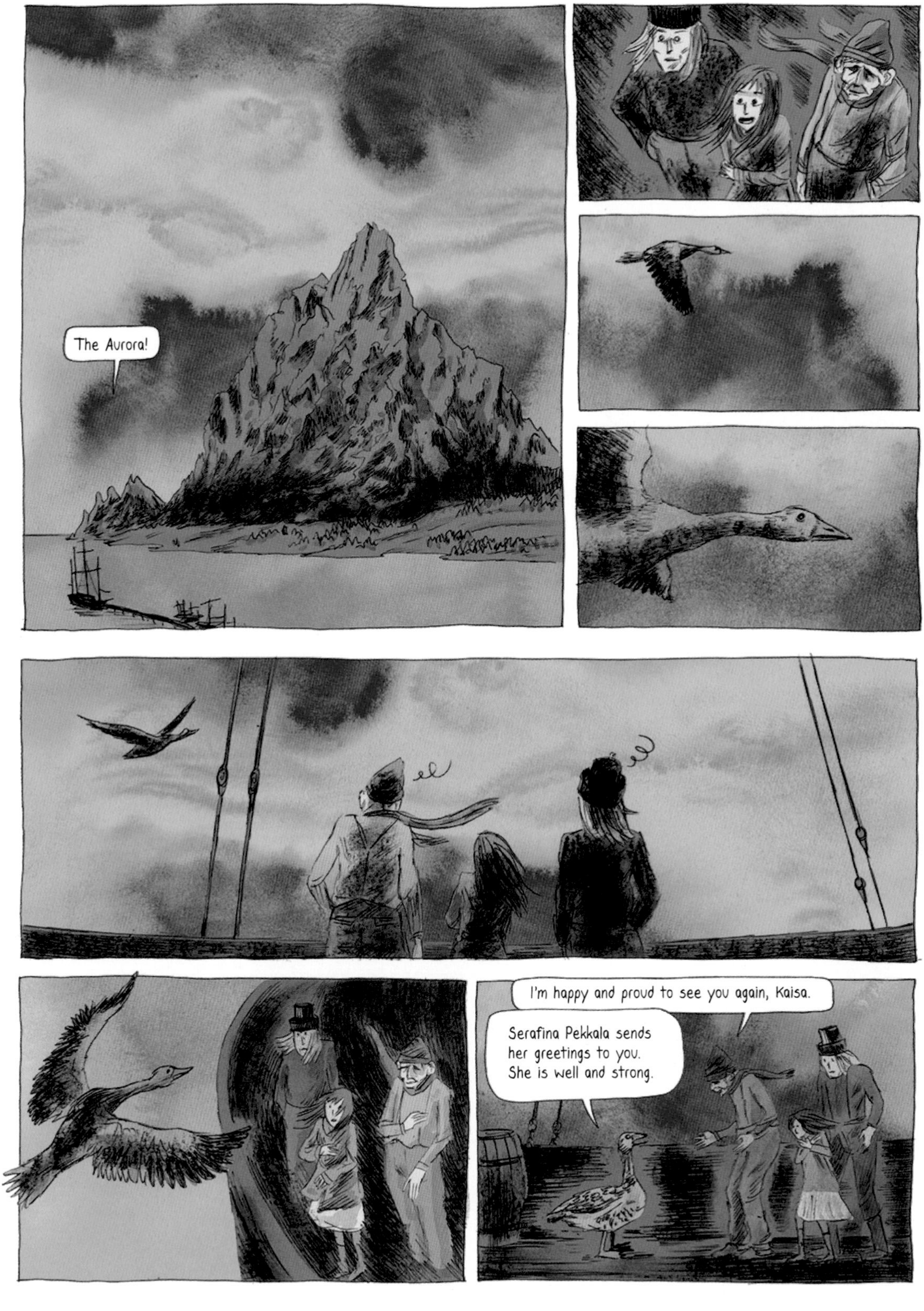
The Aurora!
I'm happy and proud to see you again, Kaisa.
Serafina Pekkala sends her greetings to you. She is well and strong.

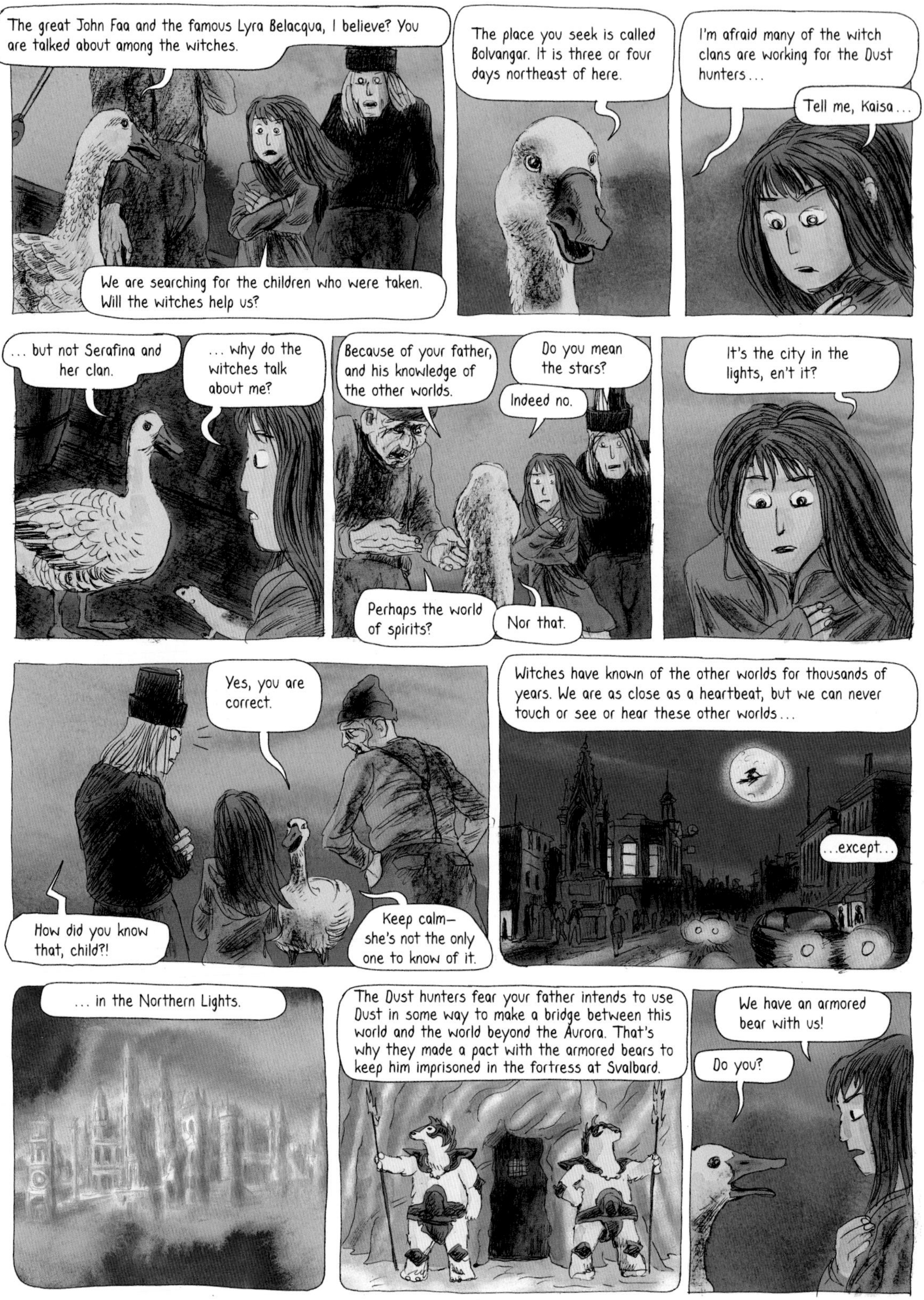
The great John Faa and the famous Lyra Belacqua, I believe? You are talked about among the witches.
We are searching for the children who were taken. Will the witches help us?
The place you seek is called Bolvangar. It is three or four days northeast of here.
I'm afraid many of the witch clans are working for the Dust hunters...
Tell me, Kaisa...
... but not Serafina and her clan.
... why do the witches talk about me?
Because of your father, and his knowledge of the other worlds.
Do you mean the stars?
Indeed no.
Perhaps the world of spirits?
Nor that.
It's the city in the lights, en't it?
Yes, you are correct.
How did you know that, child?!
Keep calm—she's not the only one to know of it.
Witches have known of the other worlds for thousands of years. We are as close as a heartbeat, but we can never touch or see or hear these other worlds...
...except...
... in the Northern Lights.
The Dust hunters fear your father intends to use Dust in some way to make a bridge between this world and the world beyond the Aurora. That's why they made a pact with the armored bears to keep him imprisoned in the fortress at Svalbard.
We have an armored bear with us!
Do you?

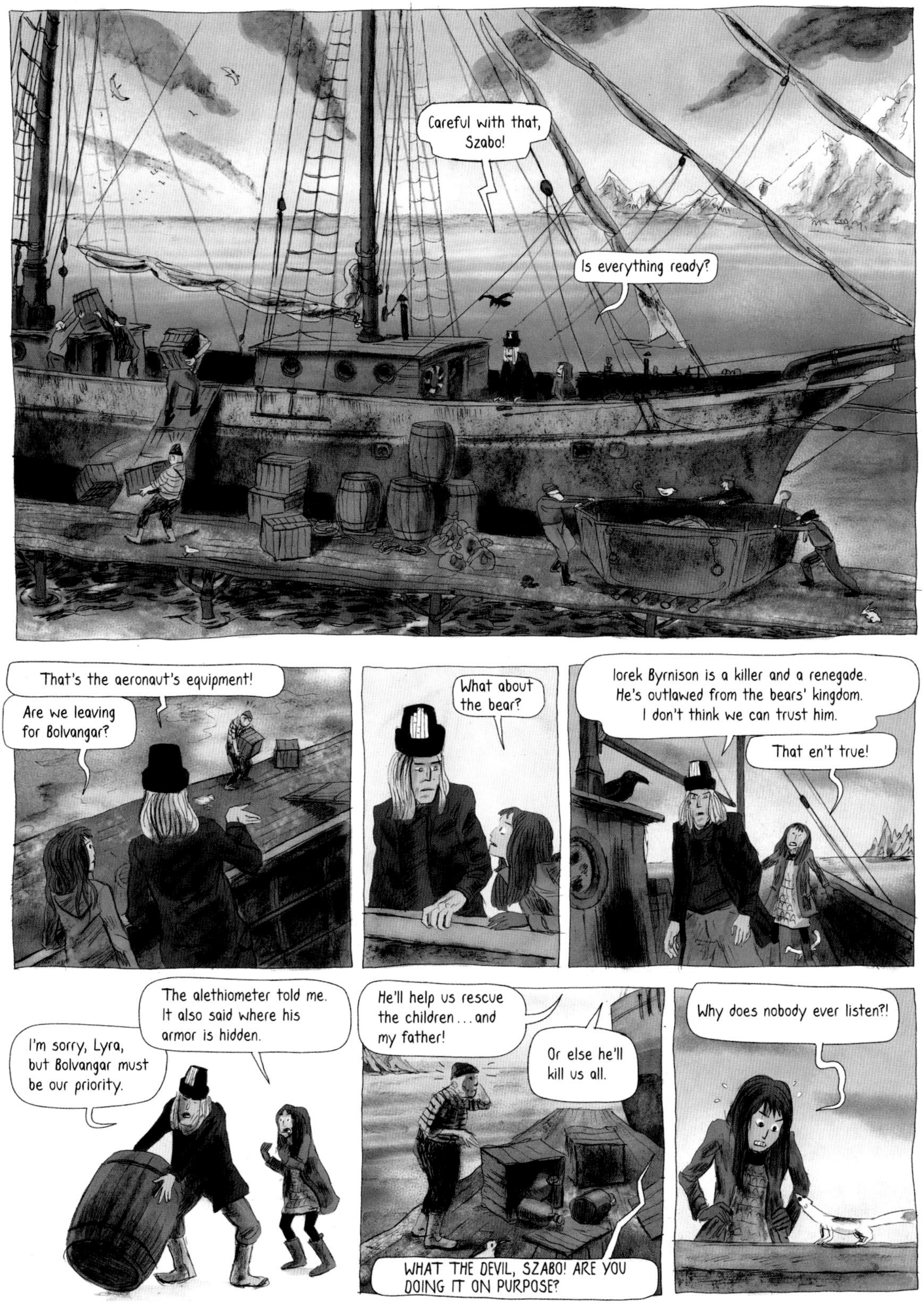
Careful with that, Szabo!
Is everything ready?
That's the aeronaut's equipment!
Are we leaving for Bolvangar?
What about the bear?
Iorek Byrnison is a killer and a renegade. He's outlawed from the bears' kingdom. I don't think we can trust him.
That en't true!
I'm sorry, Lyra, but Bolvangar must be our priority.
The alethiometer told me. It also said where his armor is hidden.
He'll help us rescue the children... and my father!
Or else he'll kill us all.
WHAT THE DEVIL, SZABO! ARE YOU DOING IT ON PURPOSE?
Why does nobody ever listen?!

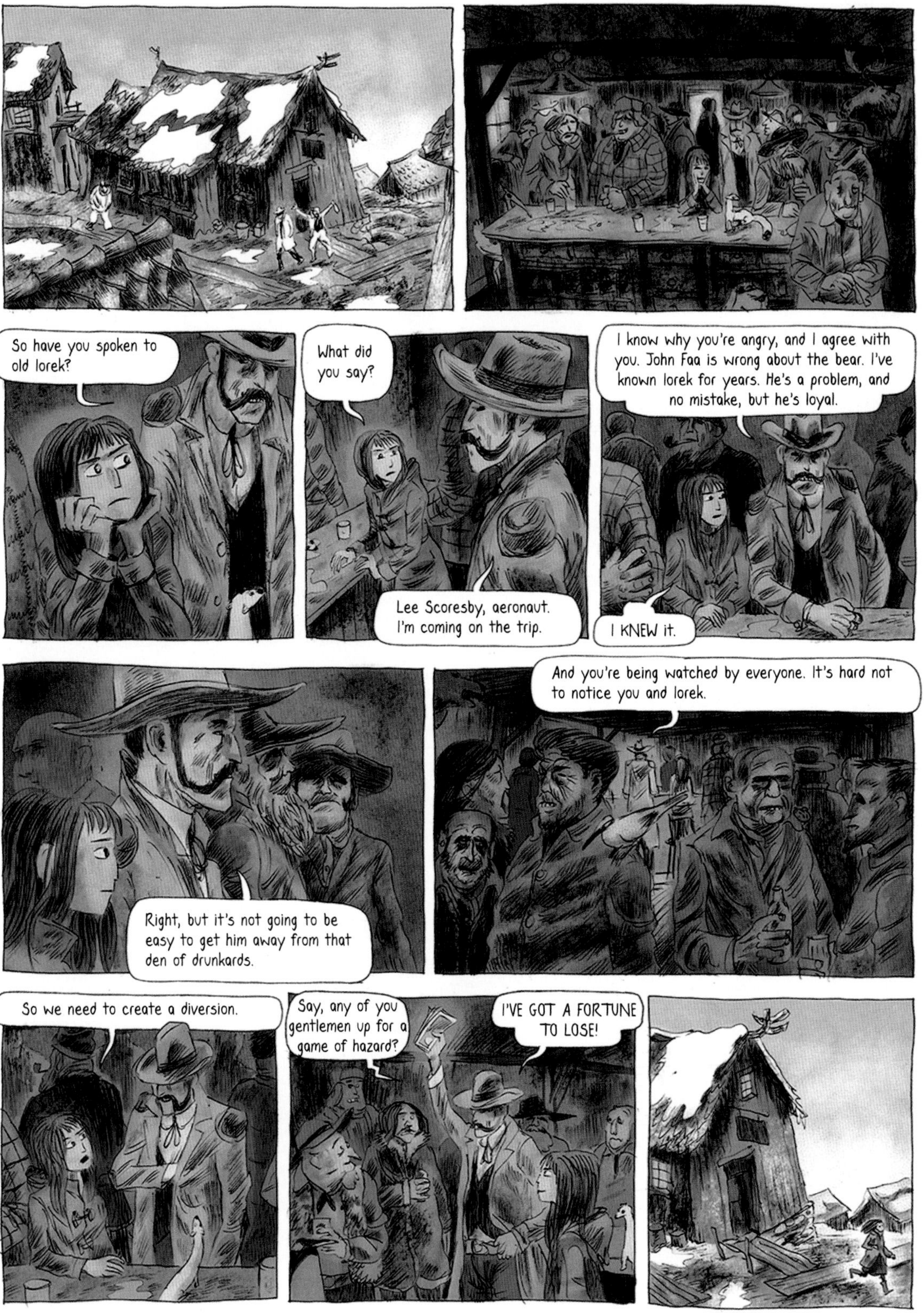
So have you spoken to old Iorek?
What did you say?
Lee Scoresby, aeronaut. I'm coming on the trip.
I know why you're angry, and I agree with you. John Faa is wrong about the bear. I've known Iorek for years. He's a problem, and no mistake, but he's loyal.
I KNEW it.
Right, but it's not going to be easy to get him away from that den of drunkards.
And you're being watched by everyone. It's hard not to notice you and Iorek.
So we need to create a diversion.
Say, any of you gentlemen up for a game of hazard?
I'VE GOT A FORTUNE TO LOSE!

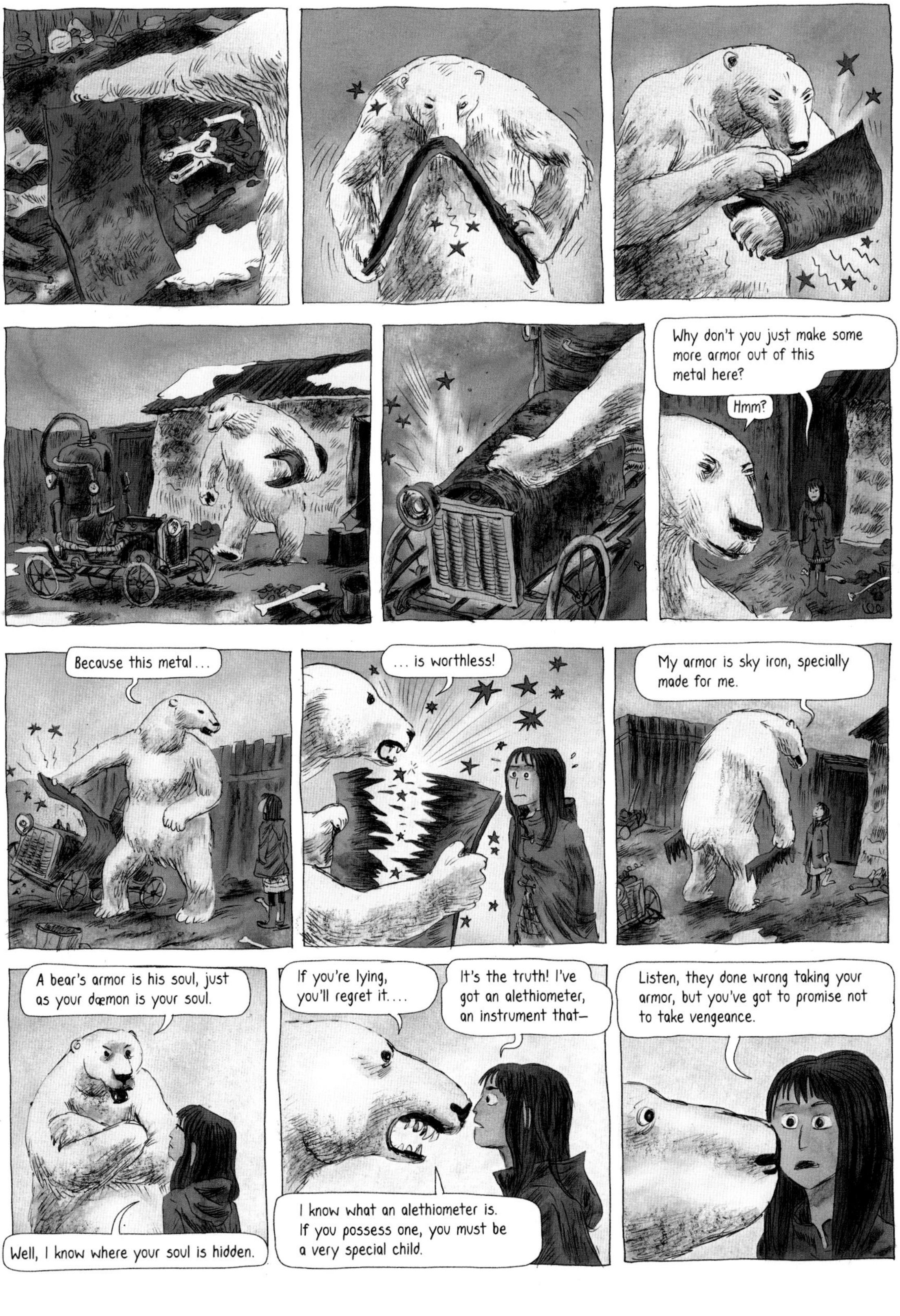
Why don't you just make some more armor out of this metal here?
Hmm?
Because this metal...
... is worthless!
My armor is sky iron, specially made for me.
A bear's armor is his soul, just as your dæmon is your soul.
Well, I know where your soul is hidden.
If you're lying, you'll regret it....
It's the truth! I've got an alethiometer, an instrument that—
I know what an alethiometer is. If you possess one, you must be a very special child.
Listen, they done wrong taking your armor, but you've got to promise not to take vengeance.

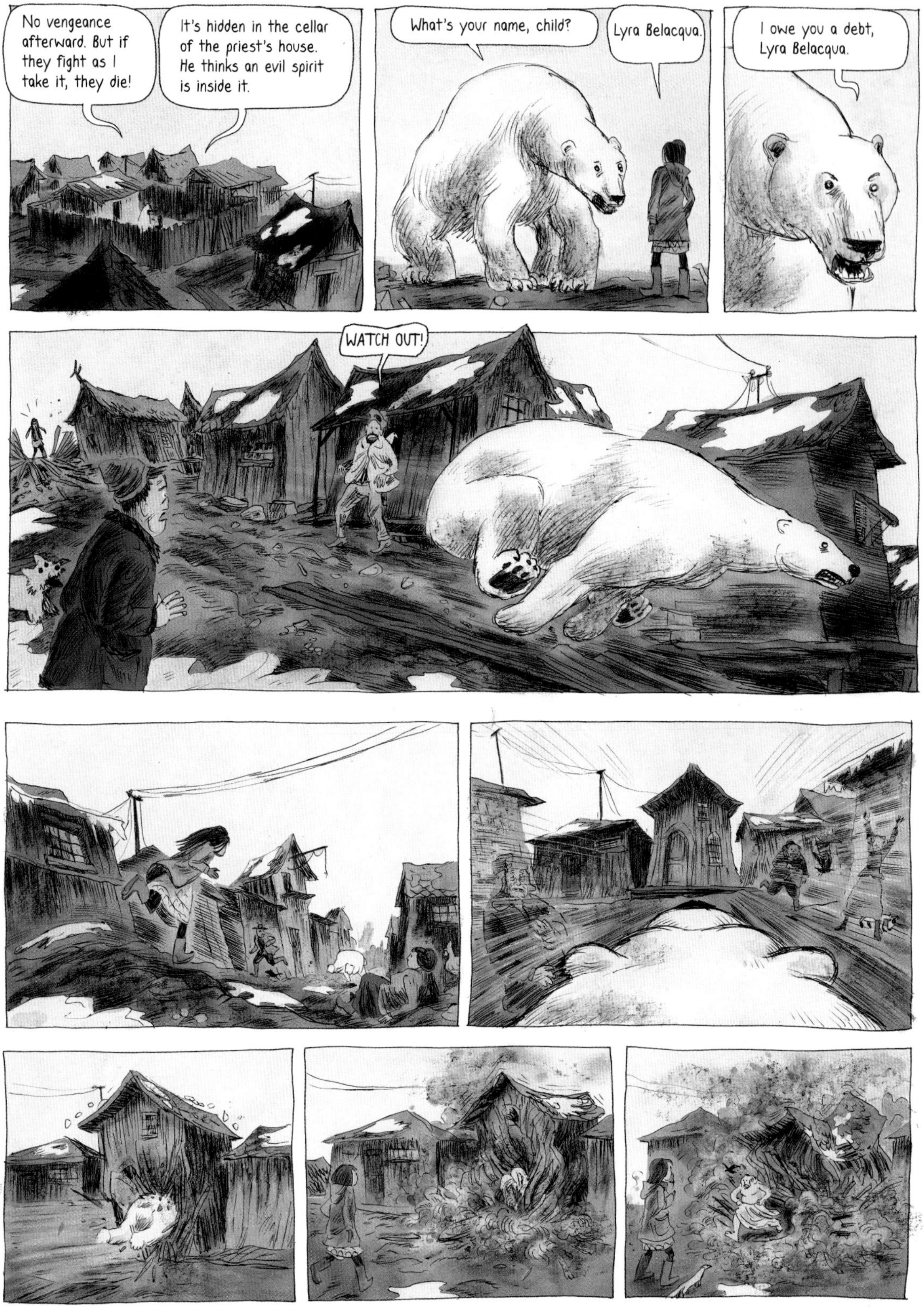
No vengeance afterward. But if they fight as I take it, they die!
It's hidden in the cellar of the priest's house. He thinks an evil spirit is inside it.
What's your name, child?
Lyra Belacqua.
I owe you a debt, Lyra Belacqua.
WATCH OUT!

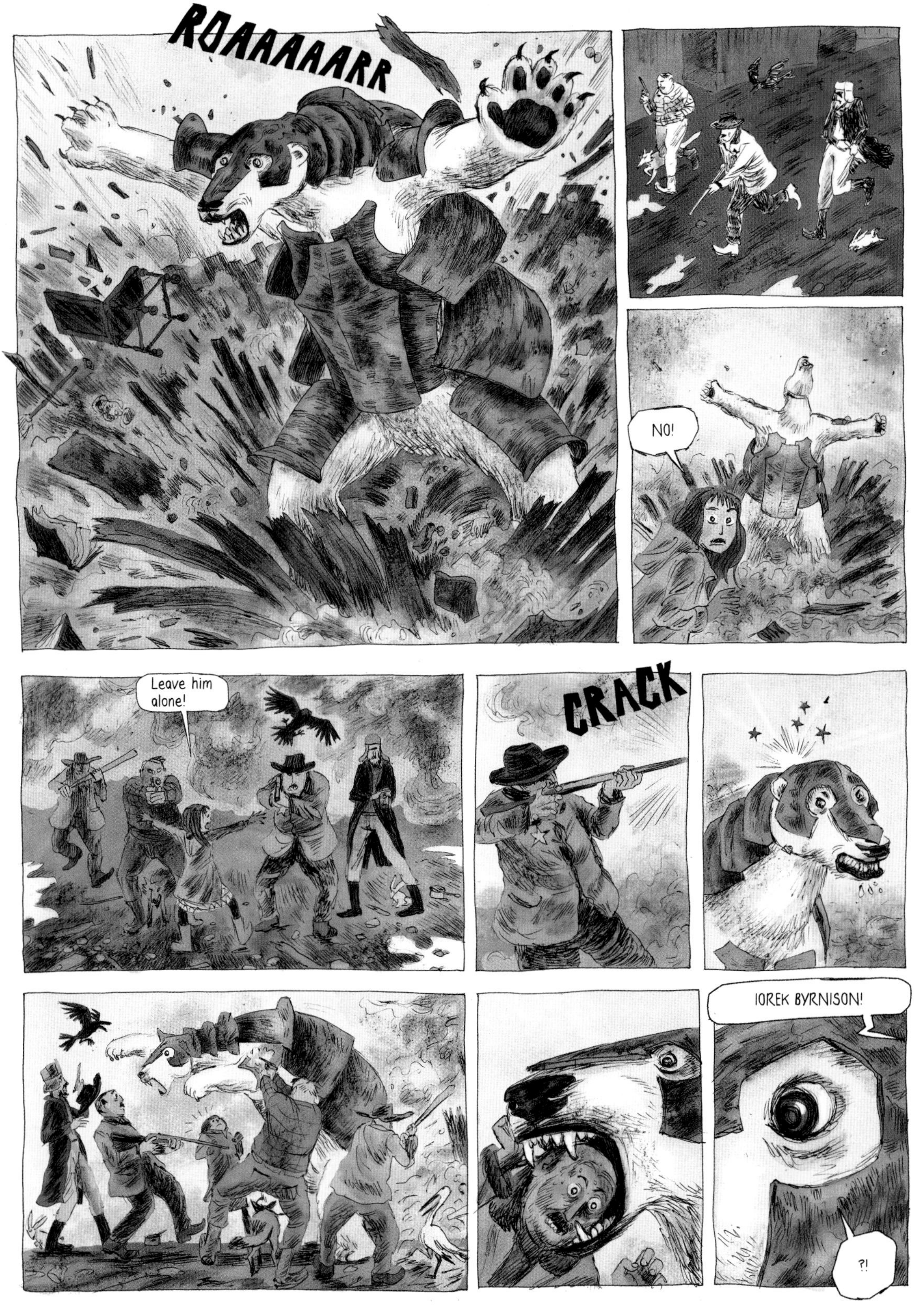
ROAAAAAARR
NO!
Leave him alone!
CRACK
IOREK BYRNISON!
?!

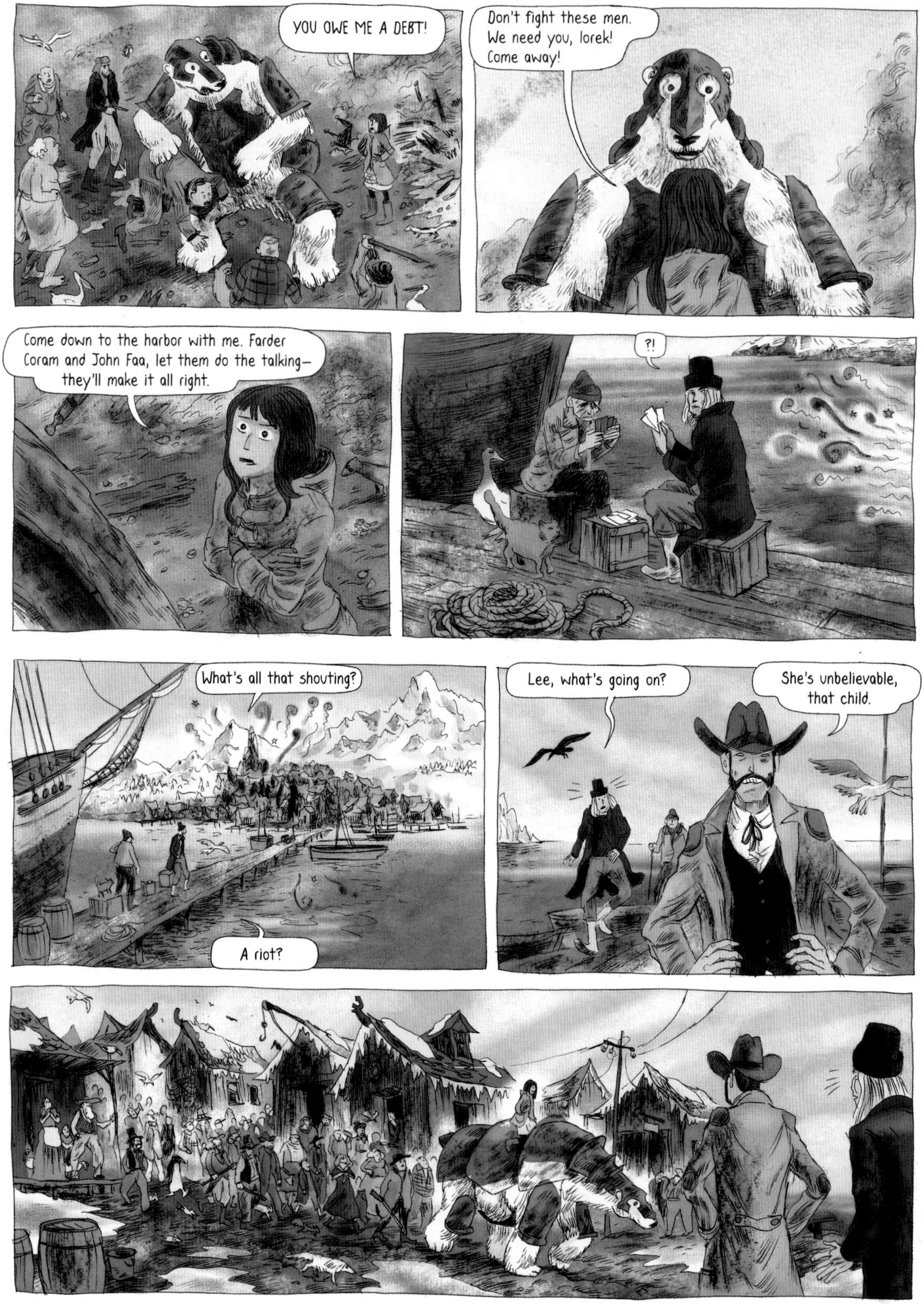
YOU OWE ME A DEBT!
Don't fight these men. We need you, Iorek! Come away!
Come down to the harbor with me. Farder Coram and John Faa, let them do the talking—they'll make it all right.
?!
What's all that shouting?
A riot?
Lee, what's going on?
She's unbelievable, that child.

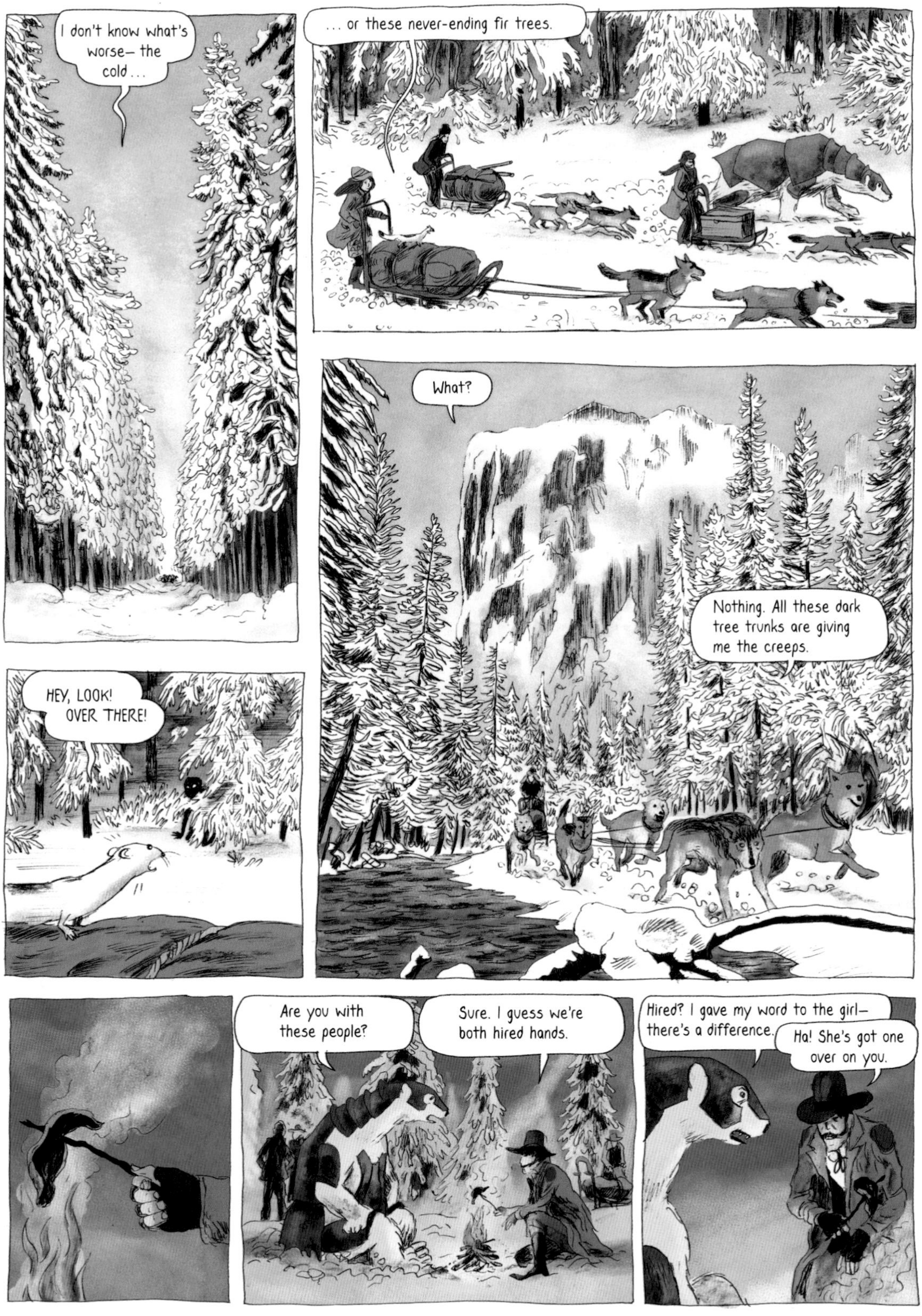
I don't know what's worse— the cold . . .
. . . or these never-ending fir trees.
What?
Nothing. All these dark tree trunks are giving me the creeps.
HEY, LOOK! OVER THERE!
Are you with these people?
Sure. I guess we're both hired hands.
Hired? I gave my word to the girl— there's a difference.
Ha! She's got one over on you.

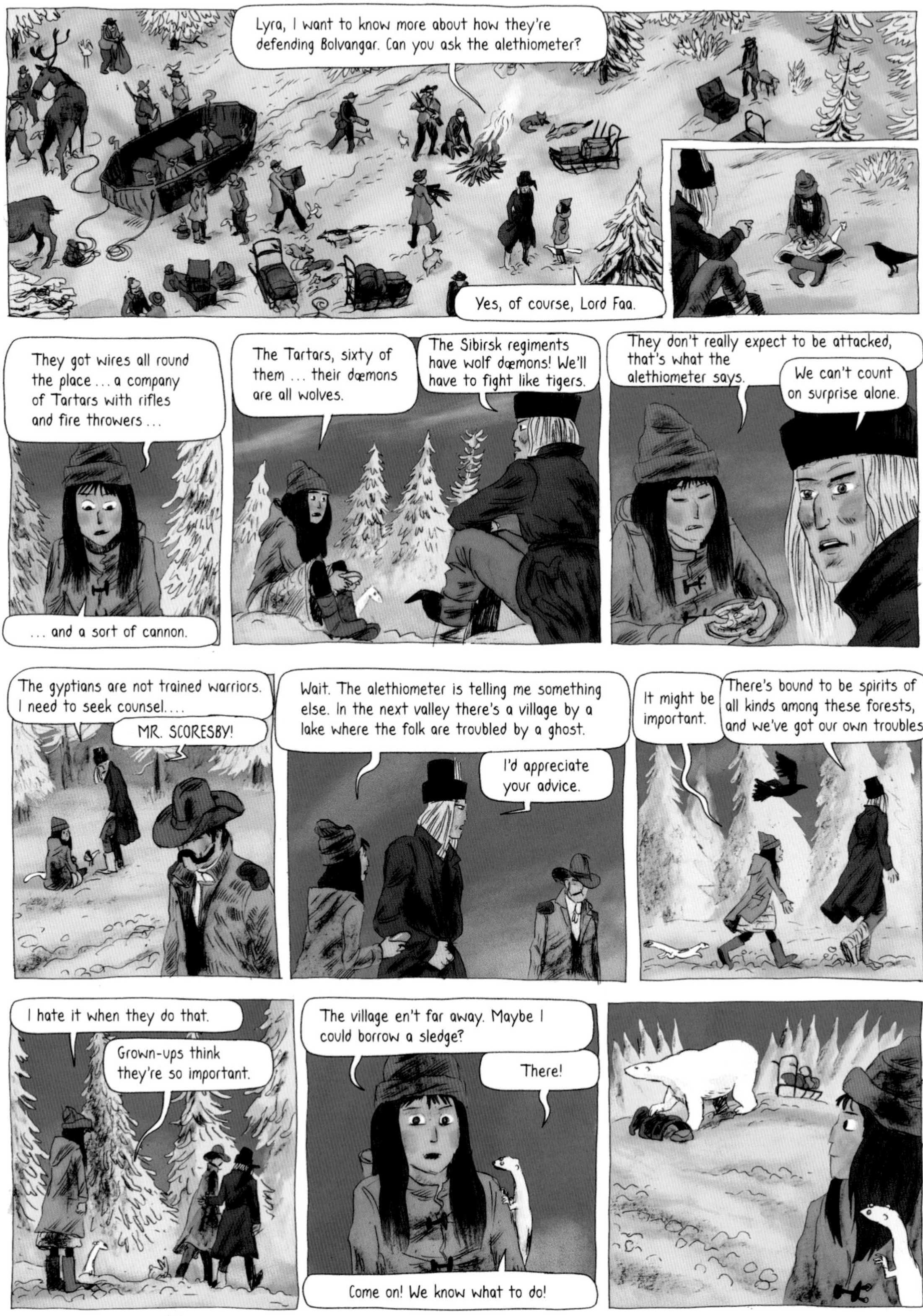
Lyra, I want to know more about how they're defending Bolvangar. Can you ask the alethiometer?
Yes, of course, Lord Faa.
They got wires all round the place . . . a company of Tartars with rifles and fire throwers . . .
. . . and a sort of cannon.
The Tartars, sixty of them . . . their dæmons are all wolves.
The Sibirsk regiments have wolf dæmons! We'll have to fight like tigers.
They don't really expect to be attacked, that's what the alethiometer says.
We can't count on surprise alone.
The gyptians are not trained warriors. I need to seek counsel. . . .
MR. SCORESBY!
Wait. The alethiometer is telling me something else. In the next valley there's a village by a lake where the folk are troubled by a ghost.
I'd appreciate your advice.
It might be important.
There's bound to be spirits of all kinds among these forests, and we've got our own troubles.
I hate it when they do that.
Grown-ups think they're so important.
The village en't far away. Maybe I could borrow a sledge?
There!
Come on! We know what to do!

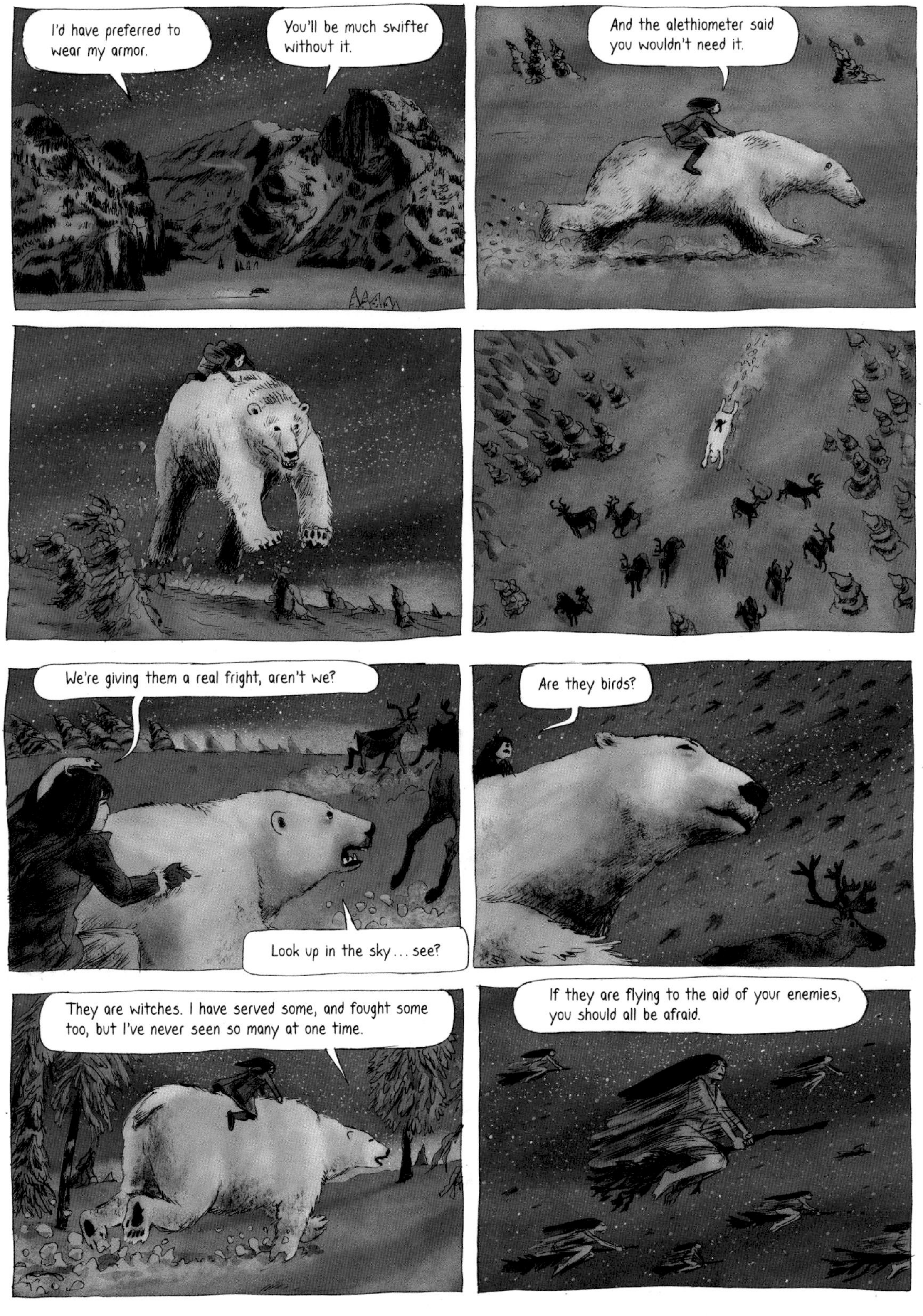
I'd have preferred to wear my armor.
You'll be much swifter without it.
And the alethiometer said you wouldn't need it.
We're giving them a real fright, aren't we?
Look up in the sky... see?
Are they birds?
They are witches. I have served some, and fought some too, but I've never seen so many at one time.
If they are flying to the aid of your enemies, you should all be afraid.

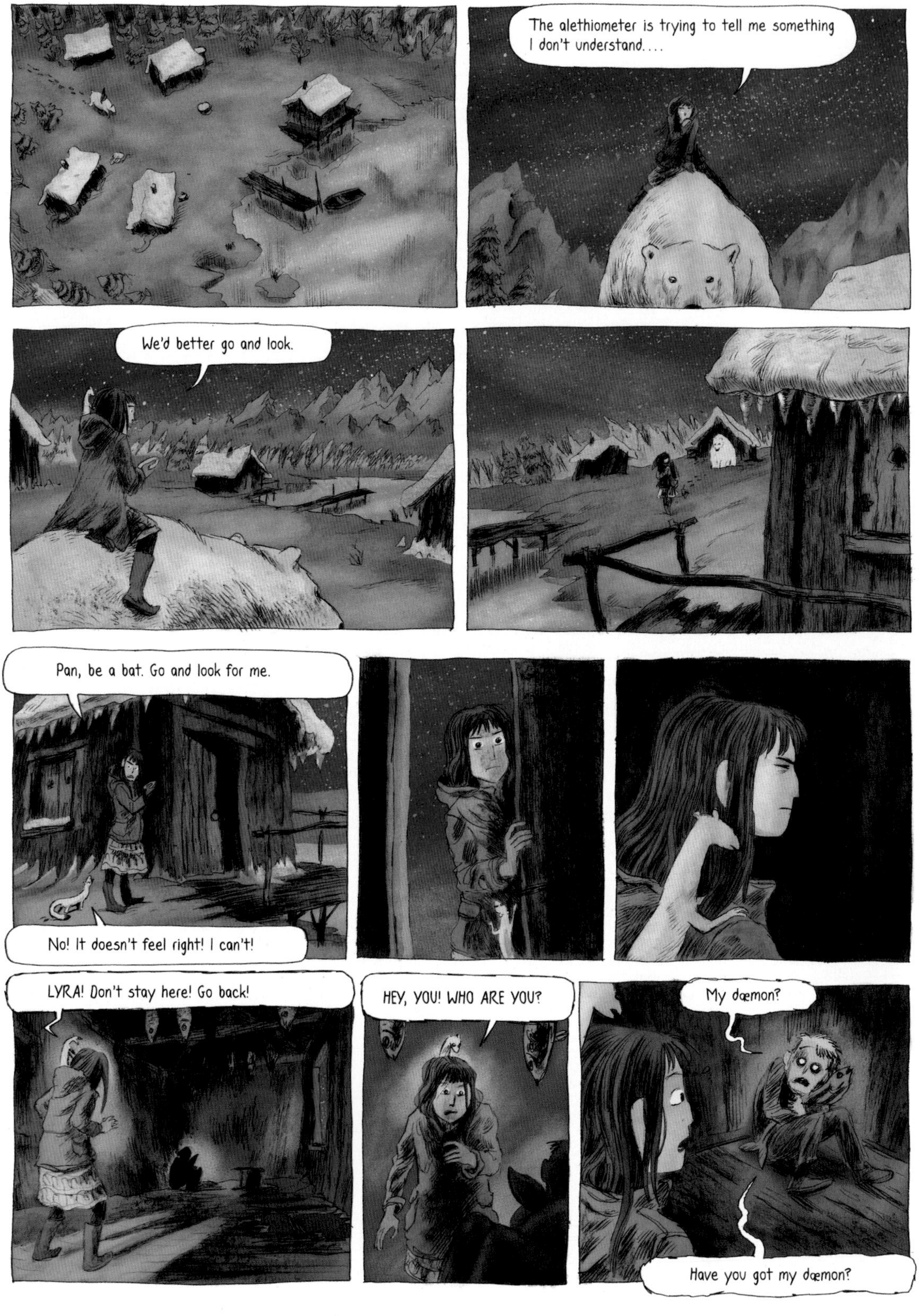
The alethiometer is trying to tell me something I don't understand. . . .
We'd better go and look.
Pan, be a bat. Go and look for me.
No! It doesn't feel right! I can't!
LYRA! Don't stay here! Go back!
HEY, YOU! WHO ARE YOU?
My dæmon?
Have you got my dæmon?

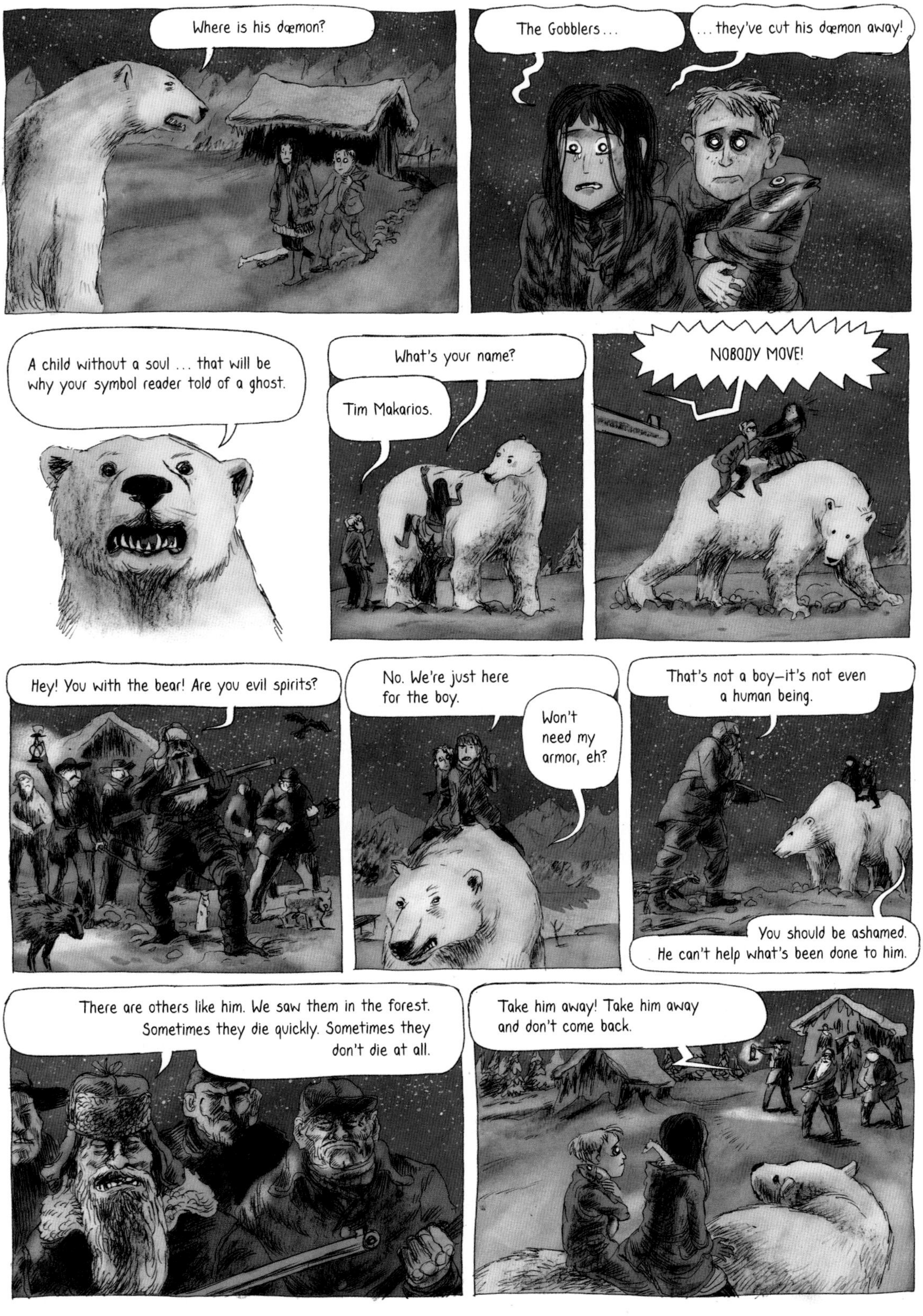
Where is his dæmon?
The Gobblers . . .
. . . they've cut his dæmon away!
A child without a soul . . . that will be why your symbol reader told of a ghost.
What's your name?
Tim Makarios.
NOBODY MOVE!
Hey! You with the bear! Are you evil spirits?
No. We're just here for the boy.
Won't need my armor, eh?
That's not a boy—it's not even a human being.
You should be ashamed. He can't help what's been done to him.
There are others like him. We saw them in the forest. Sometimes they die quickly. Sometimes they don't die at all.
Take him away! Take him away and don't come back.

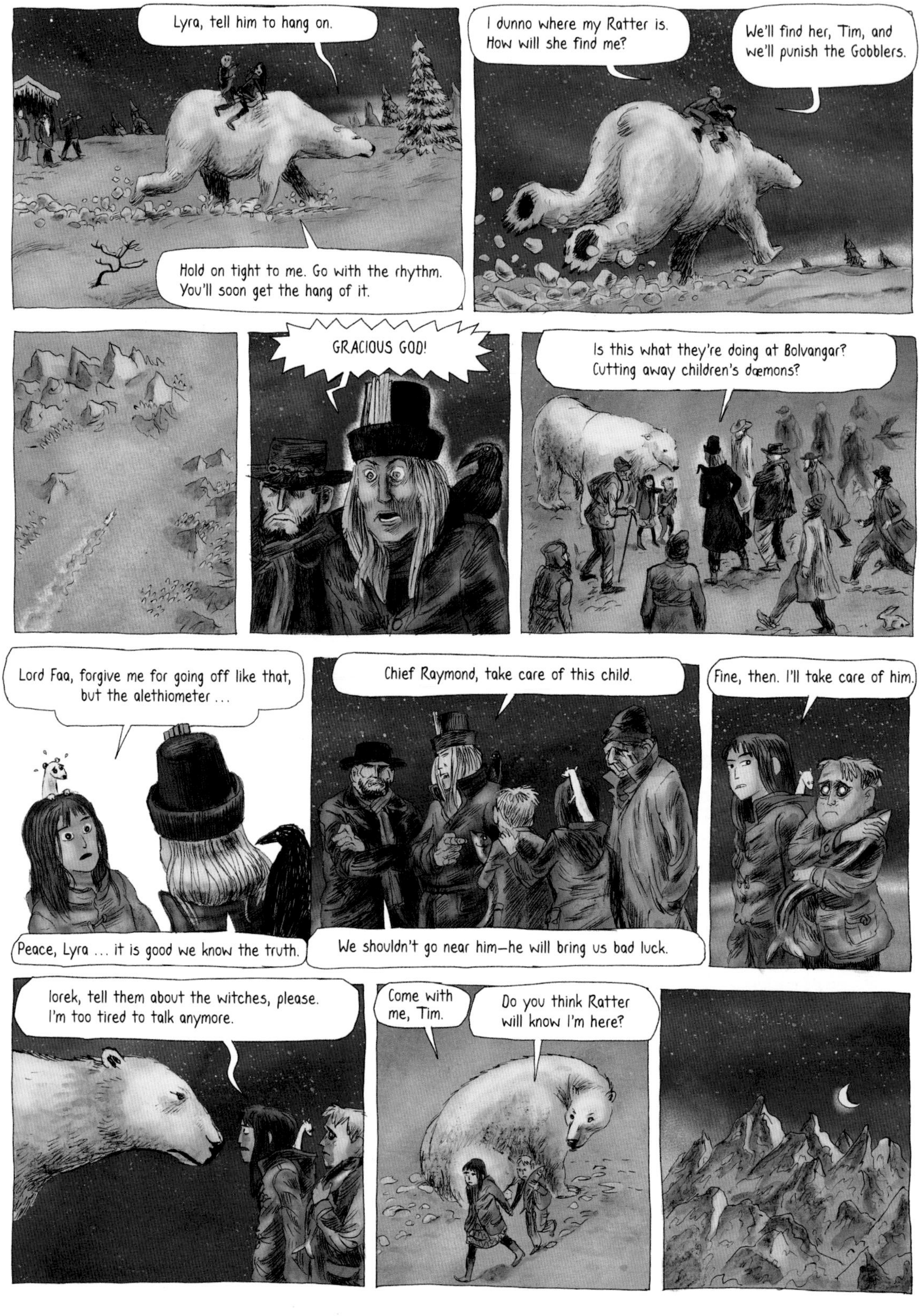
Lyra, tell him to hang on.
Hold on tight to me. Go with the rhythm. You'll soon get the hang of it.
I dunno where my Ratter is. How will she find me?
We'll find her, Tim, and we'll punish the Gobblers.
GRACIOUS GOD!
Is this what they're doing at Bolvangar? Cutting away children's dæmons?
Lord Faa, forgive me for going off like that, but the alethiometer . . .
Peace, Lyra . . . it is good we know the truth.
Chief Raymond, take care of this child.
We shouldn't go near him—he will bring us bad luck.
Fine, then. I'll take care of him.
Iorek, tell them about the witches, please. I'm too tired to talk anymore.
Come with me, Tim.
Do you think Ratter will know I'm here?

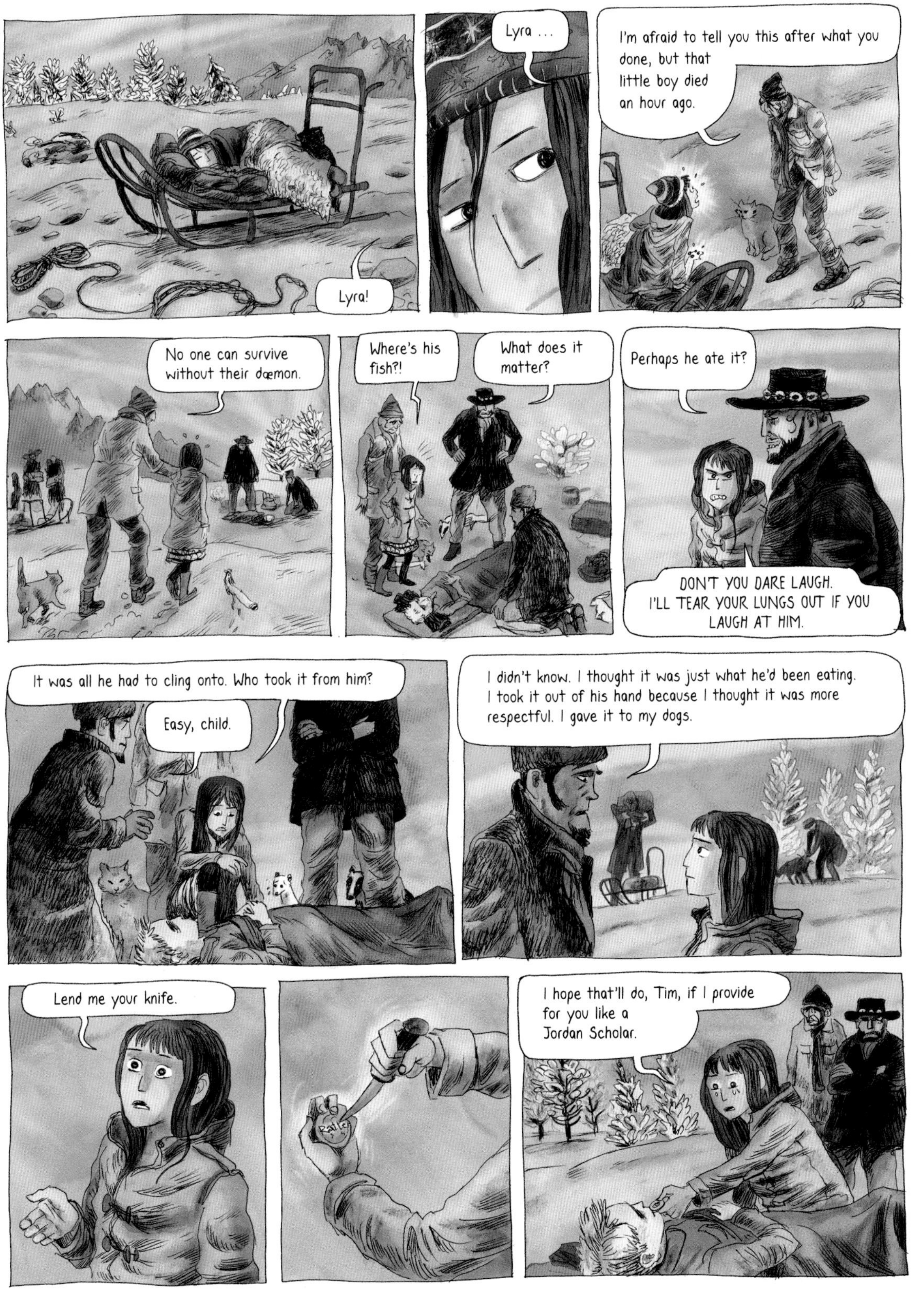
Lyra!
Lyra . . .
I'm afraid to tell you this after what you done, but that little boy died an hour ago.
No one can survive without their dæmon.
Where's his fish?!
What does it matter?
Perhaps he ate it?
DON'T YOU DARE LAUGH. I'LL TEAR YOUR LUNGS OUT IF YOU LAUGH AT HIM.
It was all he had to cling onto. Who took it from him?
Easy, child.
I didn't know. I thought it was just what he'd been eating. I took it out of his hand because I thought it was more respectful. I gave it to my dogs.
Lend me your knife.
I hope that'll do, Tim, if I provide for you like a Jordan Scholar.

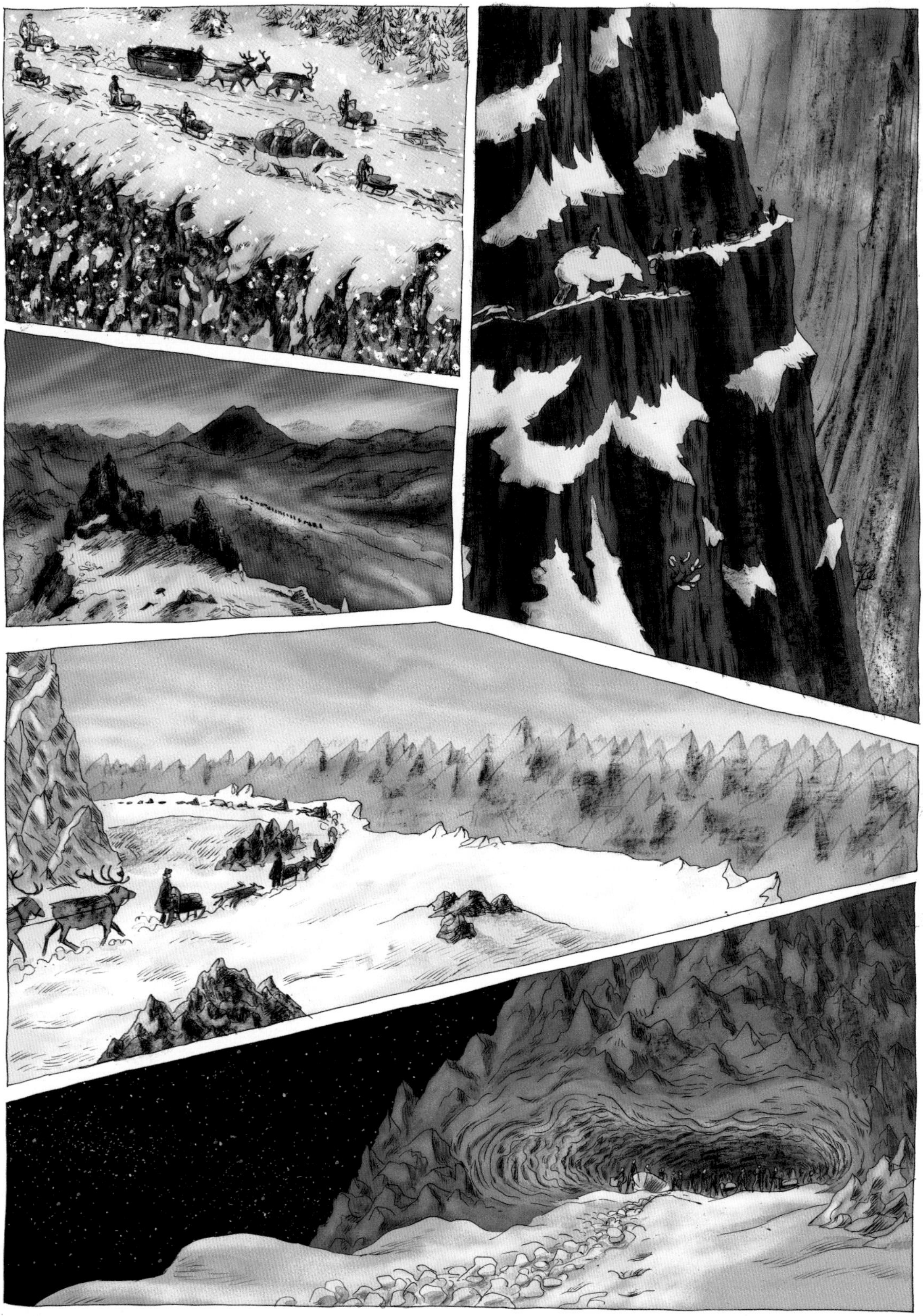

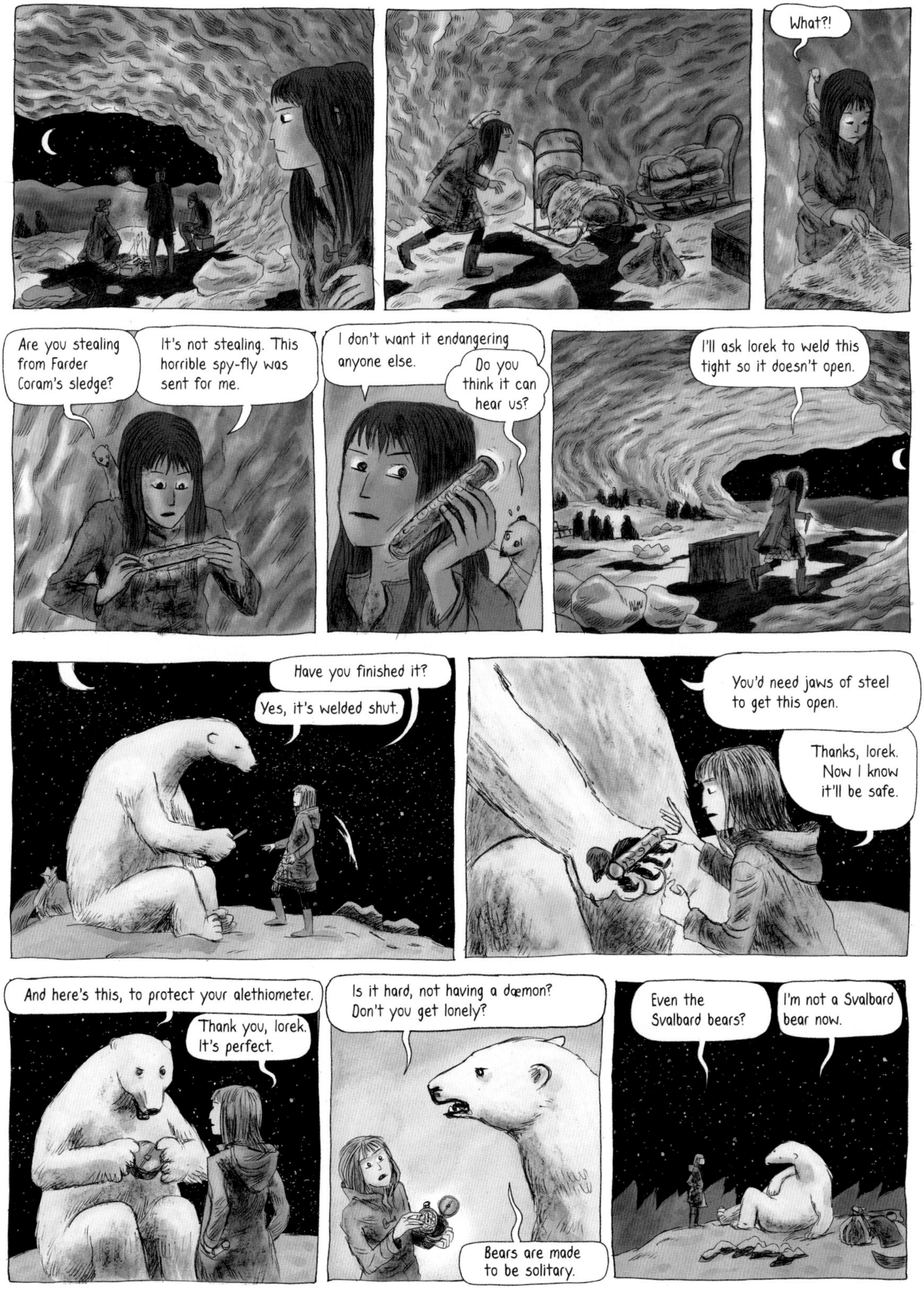
What?!
Are you stealing from Farder Coram's sledge?
It's not stealing. This horrible spy-fly was sent for me.
I don't want it endangering anyone else.
Do you think it can hear us?
I'll ask Iorek to weld this tight so it doesn't open.
Have you finished it?
Yes, it's welded shut.
You'd need jaws of steel to get this open.
Thanks, Iorek. Now I know it'll be safe.
And here's this, to protect your alethiometer.
Thank you, Iorek. It's perfect.
Is it hard, not having a dæmon? Don't you get lonely?
Bears are made to be solitary.
Even the Svalbard bears?
I'm not a Svalbard bear now.

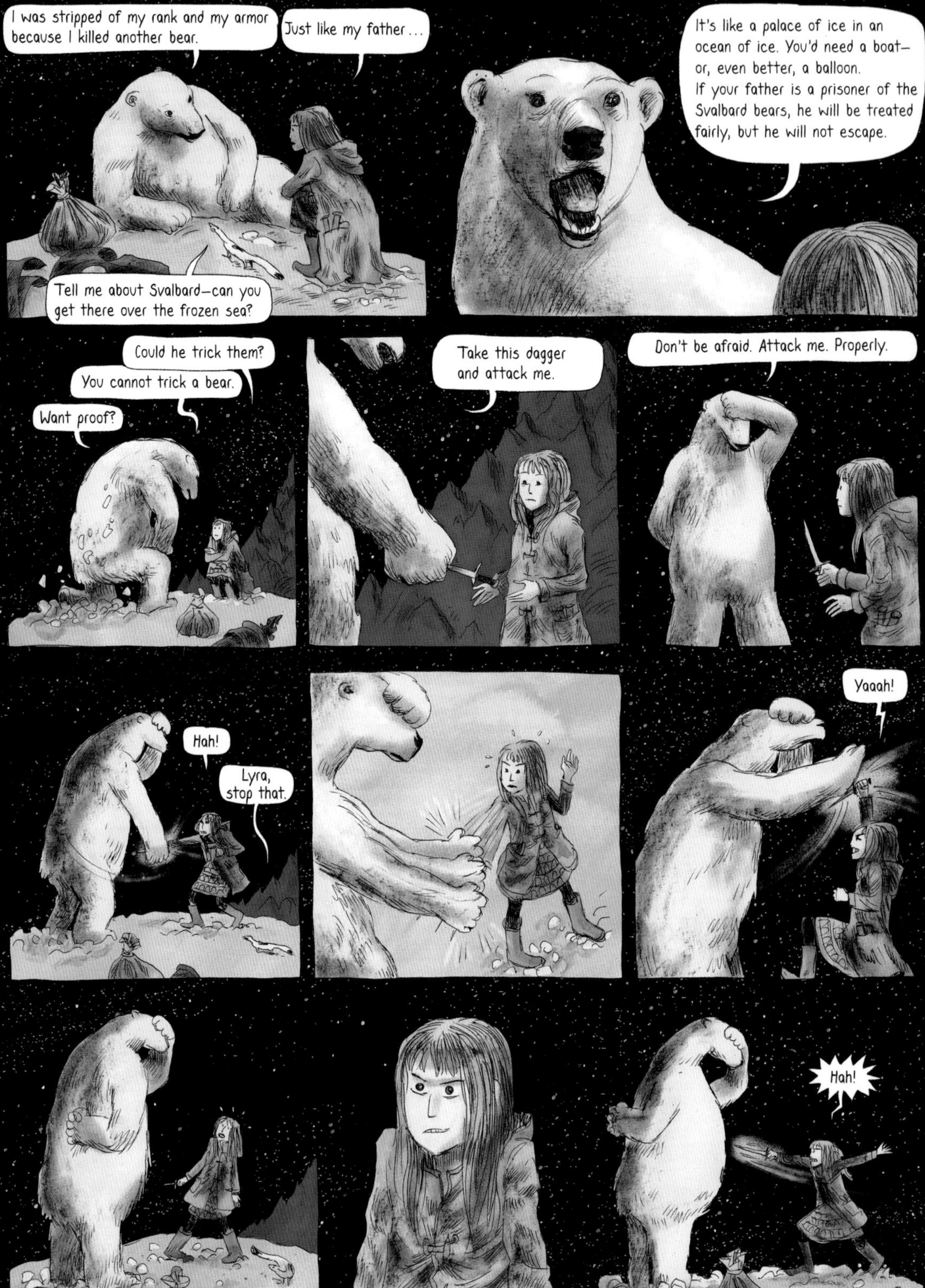
I was stripped of my rank and my armor because I killed another bear.
Just like my father...
Tell me about Svalbard—can you get there over the frozen sea?
It's like a palace of ice in an ocean of ice. You'd need a boat—or, even better, a balloon.
If your father is a prisoner of the Svalbard bears, he will be treated fairly, but he will not escape.
Could he trick them?
You cannot trick a bear.
Want proof?
Take this dagger and attack me.
Don't be afraid. Attack me. Properly.
Hah!
Lyra, stop that.
Yaaah!
Hah!

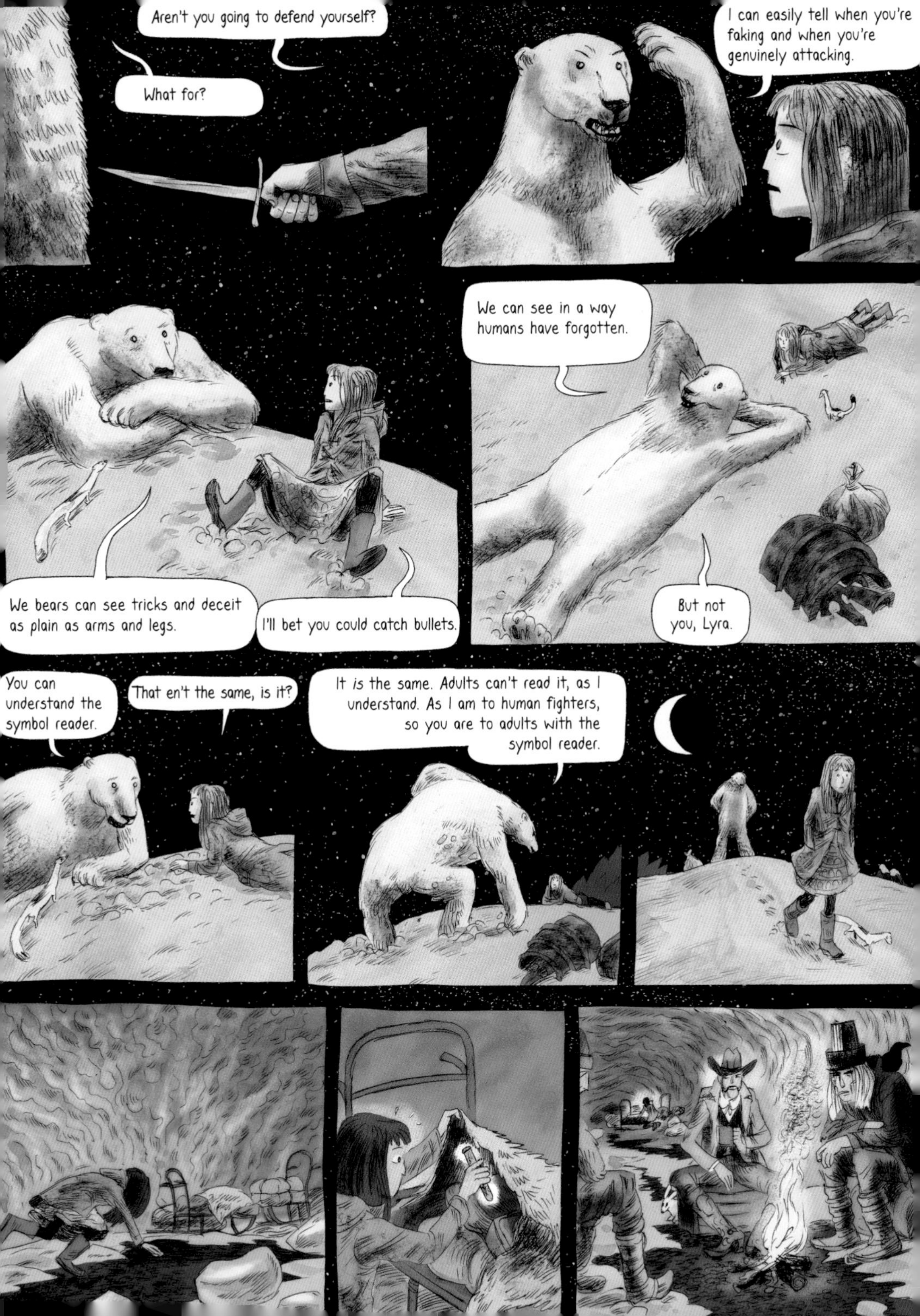
Aren't you going to defend yourself?
What for?
I can easily tell when you're faking and when you're genuinely attacking.
We bears can see tricks and deceit as plain as arms and legs.
I'll bet you could catch bullets.
We can see in a way humans have forgotten.
But not you, Lyra.
You can understand the symbol reader.
That en't the same, is it?
It *is* the same. Adults can't read it, as I understand. As I am to human fighters, so you are to adults with the symbol reader.

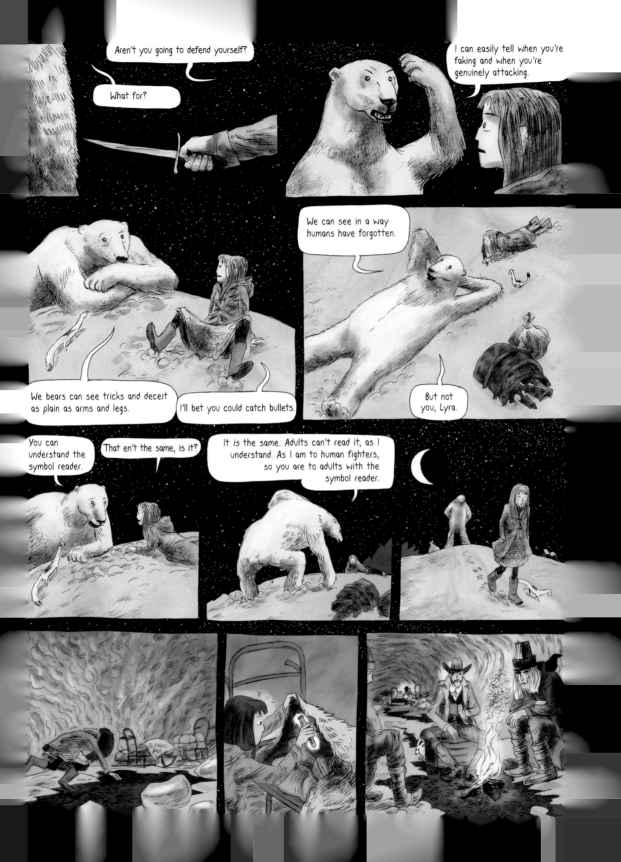

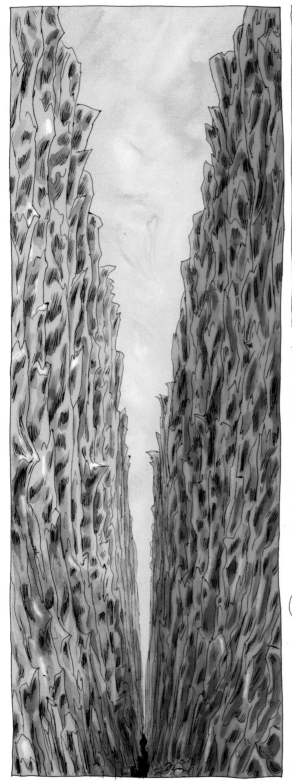

Lee...

Could you carry Iorek and his armor in your balloon?

I've done it before.

I rescued him one time from the Tartars—they had him trapped and were starving him out.

Bears aren't made to fly, but Lee saved me that day.

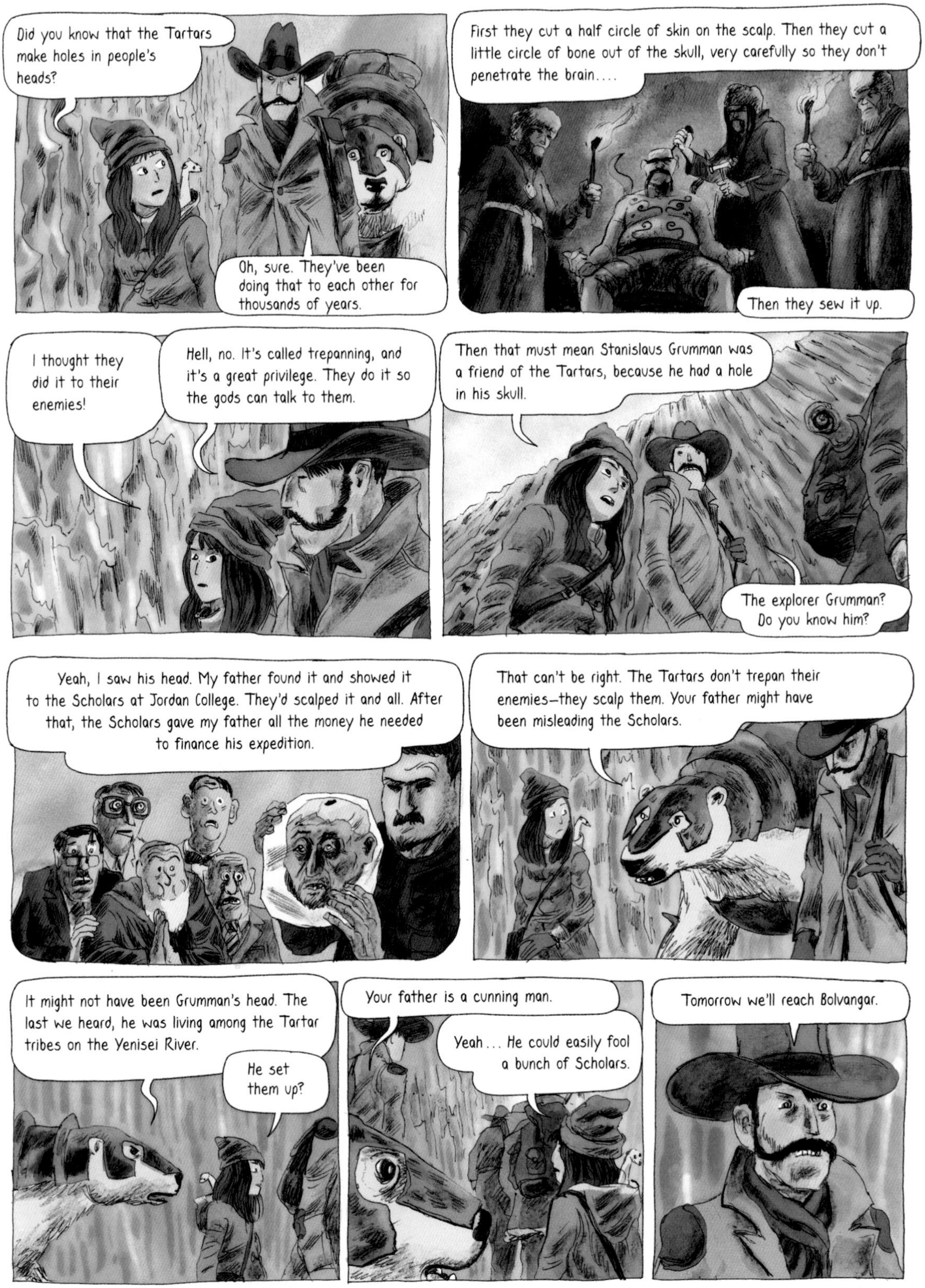
Did you know that the Tartars make holes in people's heads?
Oh, sure. They've been doing that to each other for thousands of years.
First they cut a half circle of skin on the scalp. Then they cut a little circle of bone out of the skull, very carefully so they don't penetrate the brain....
Then they sew it up.
I thought they did it to their enemies!
Hell, no. It's called trepanning, and it's a great privilege. They do it so the gods can talk to them.
Then that must mean Stanislaus Grumman was a friend of the Tartars, because he had a hole in his skull.
The explorer Grumman? Do you know him?
Yeah, I saw his head. My father found it and showed it to the Scholars at Jordan College. They'd scalped it and all. After that, the Scholars gave my father all the money he needed to finance his expedition.
That can't be right. The Tartars don't trepan their enemies—they scalp them. Your father might have been misleading the Scholars.
It might not have been Grumman's head. The last we heard, he was living among the Tartar tribes on the Yenisei River.
He set them up?
Your father is a cunning man.
Yeah... He could easily fool a bunch of Scholars.
Tomorrow we'll reach Bolvangar.

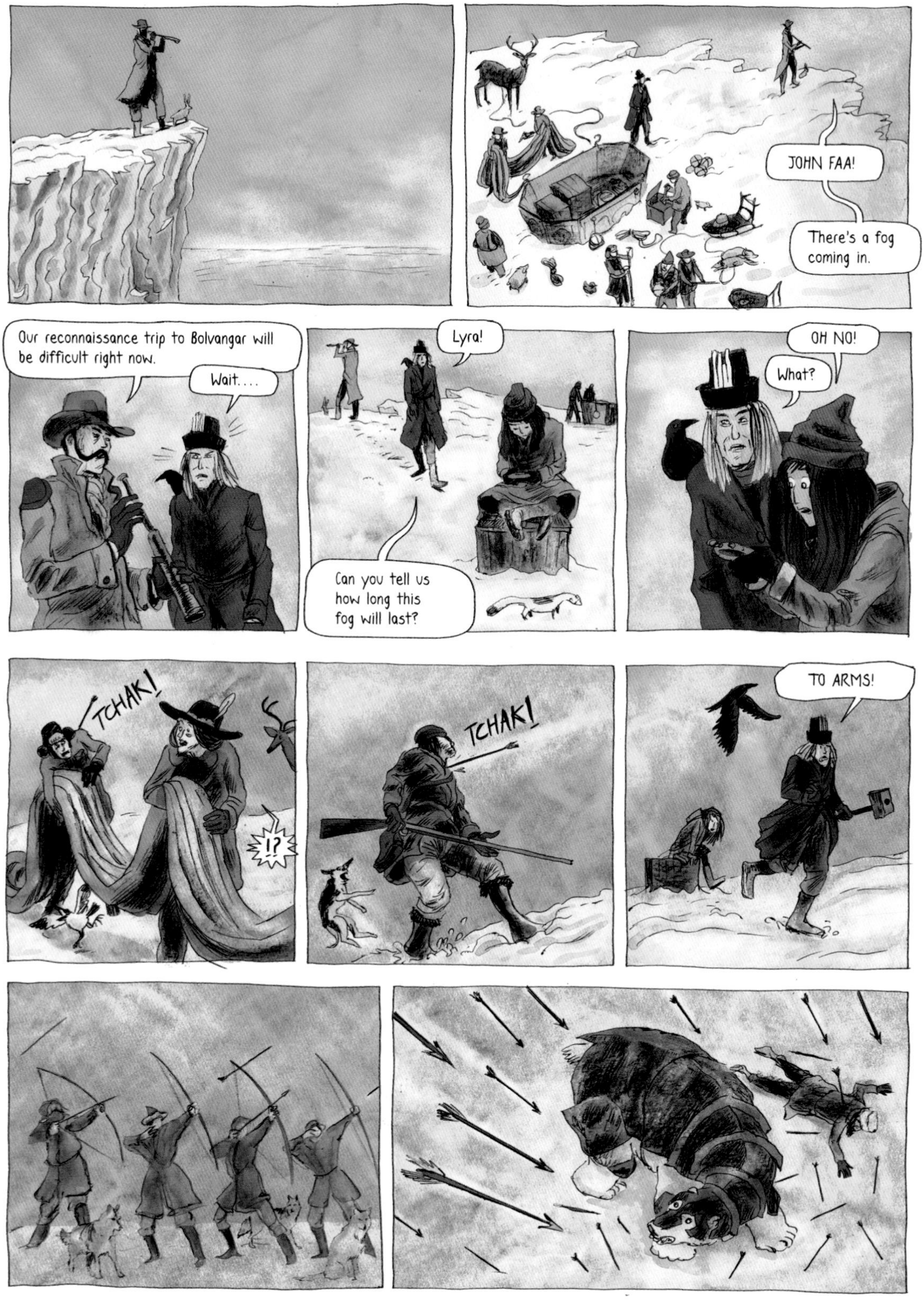
JOHN FAA!
There's a fog coming in.
Our reconnaissance trip to Bolvangar will be difficult right now.
Wait....
Lyra!
Can you tell us how long this fog will last?
OH NO!
What?
TCHAK!
!?
TCHAK!
TO ARMS!

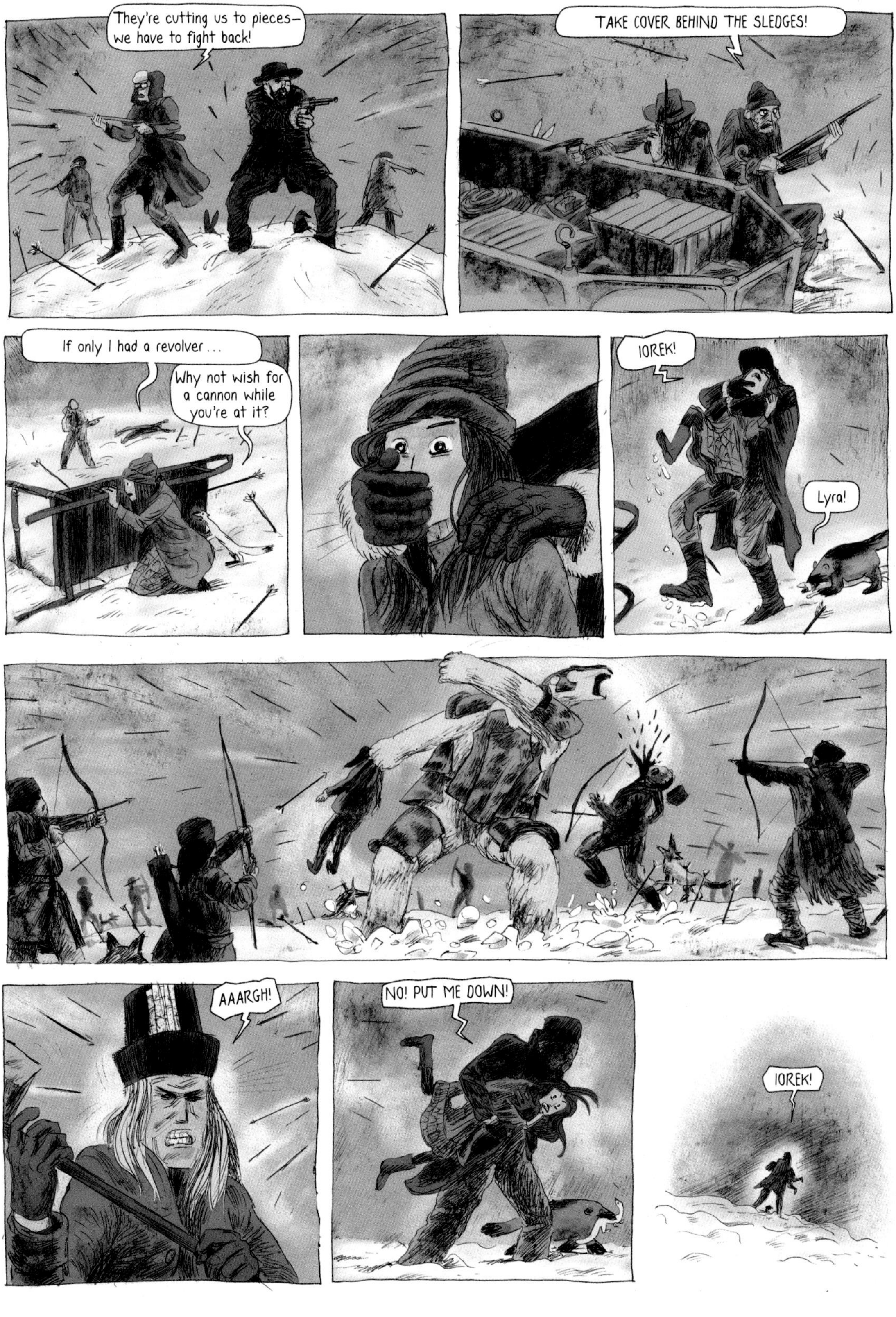
They're cutting us to pieces—we have to fight back!
TAKE COVER BEHIND THE SLEDGES!
If only I had a revolver . . .
Why not wish for a cannon while you're at it?
IOREK!
Lyra!
AAARGH!
NO! PUT ME DOWN!
IOREK!

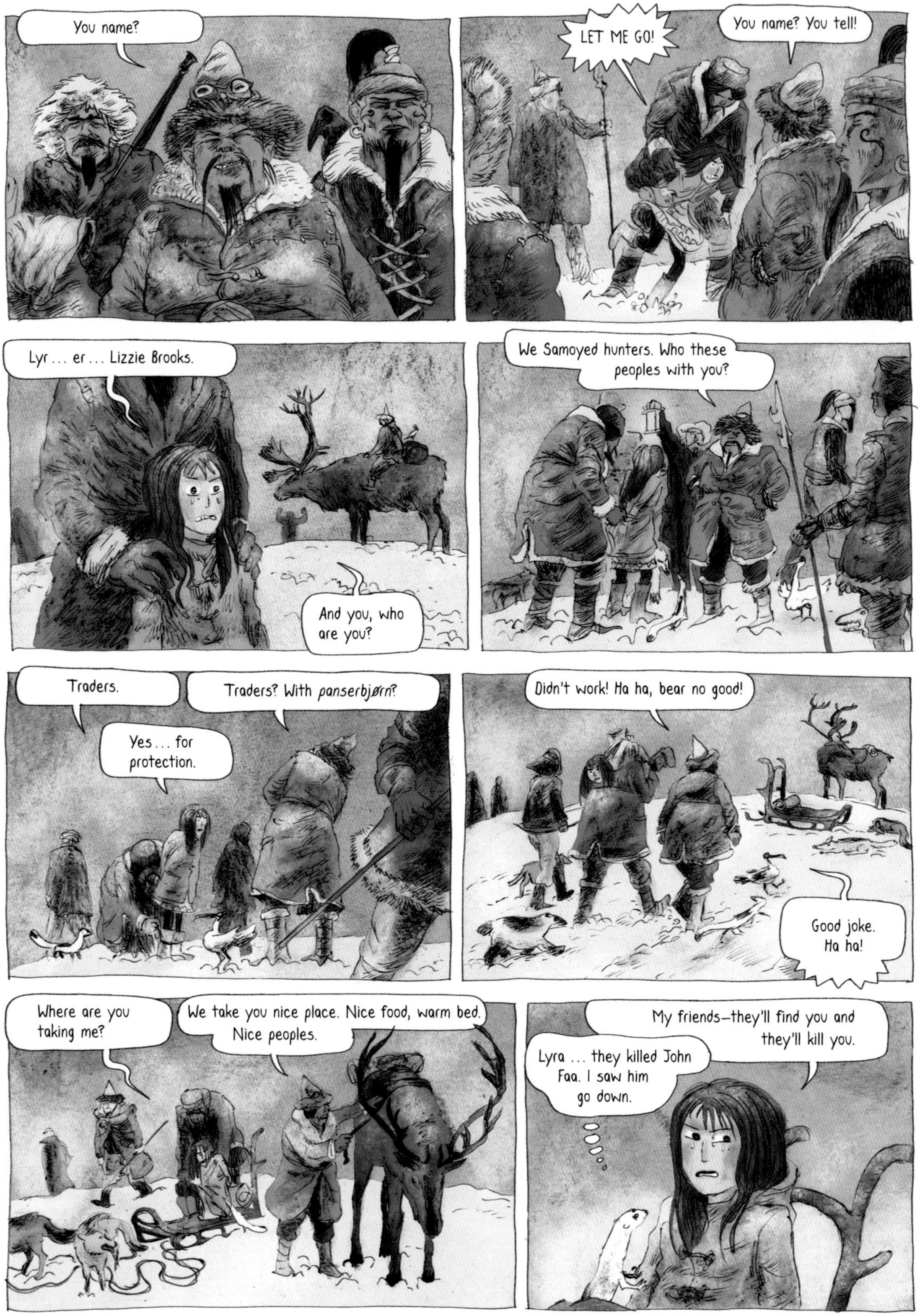
You name?
LET ME GO!
You name? You tell!
Lyr . . . er . . . Lizzie Brooks.
And you, who are you?
We Samoyed hunters. Who these peoples with you?
Traders.
Traders? With *panserbjørn*?
Yes . . . for protection.
Didn't work! Ha ha, bear no good!
Good joke. Ha ha!
Where are you taking me?
We take you nice place. Nice food, warm bed. Nice peoples.
My friends—they'll find you and they'll kill you.
Lyra . . . they killed John Faa. I saw him go down.

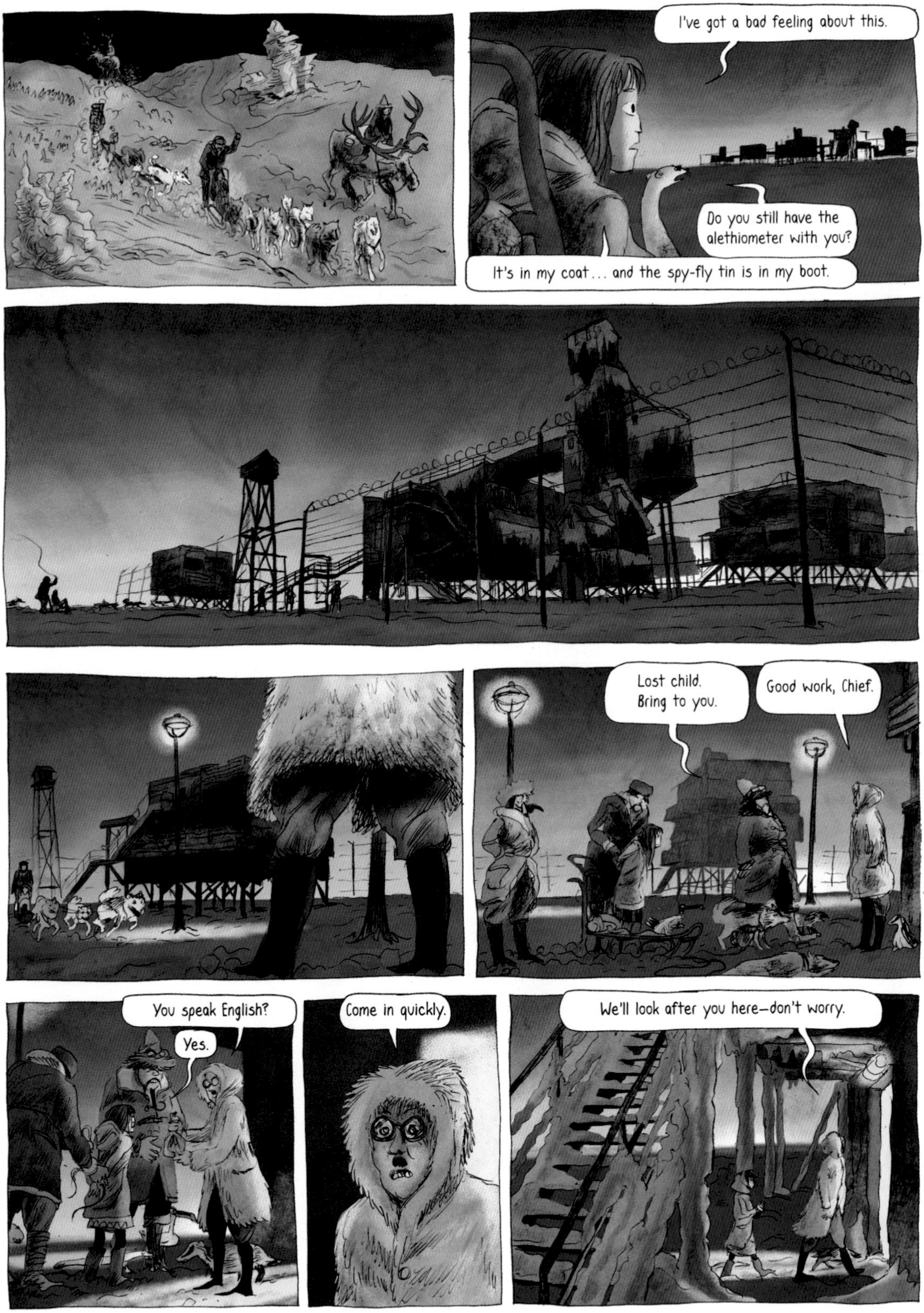
I've got a bad feeling about this.
Do you still have the alethiometer with you?
It's in my coat... and the spy-fly tin is in my boot.
Lost child. Bring to you.
Good work, Chief.
You speak English?
Yes.
Come in quickly.
We'll look after you here—don't worry.

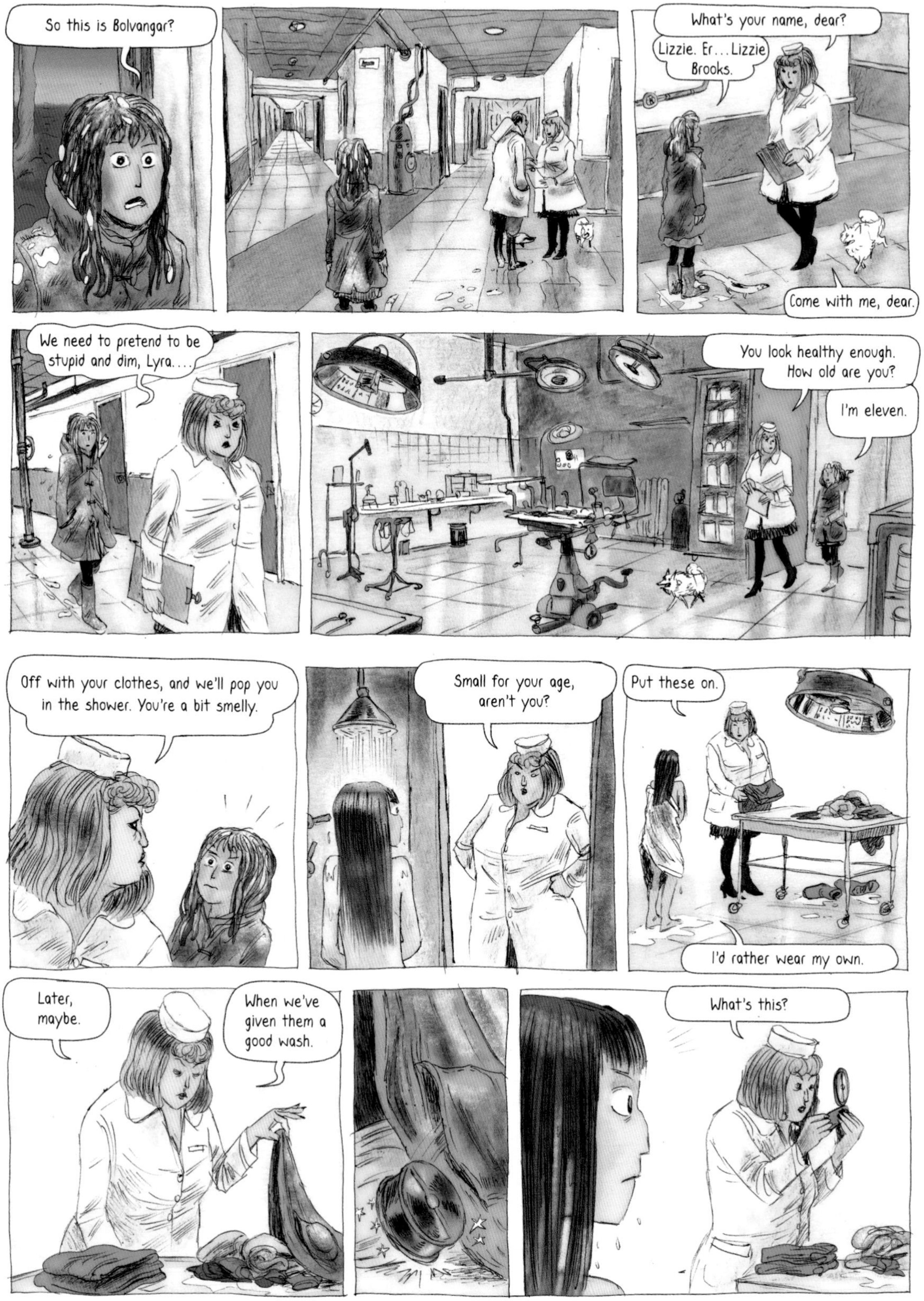
So this is Bolvangar?
What's your name, dear?
Lizzie. Er... Lizzie Brooks.
Come with me, dear.
We need to pretend to be stupid and dim, Lyra....
You look healthy enough. How old are you?
I'm eleven.
Off with your clothes, and we'll pop you in the shower. You're a bit smelly.
Small for your age, aren't you?
Put these on.
I'd rather wear my own.
Later, maybe.
When we've given them a good wash.
What's this?

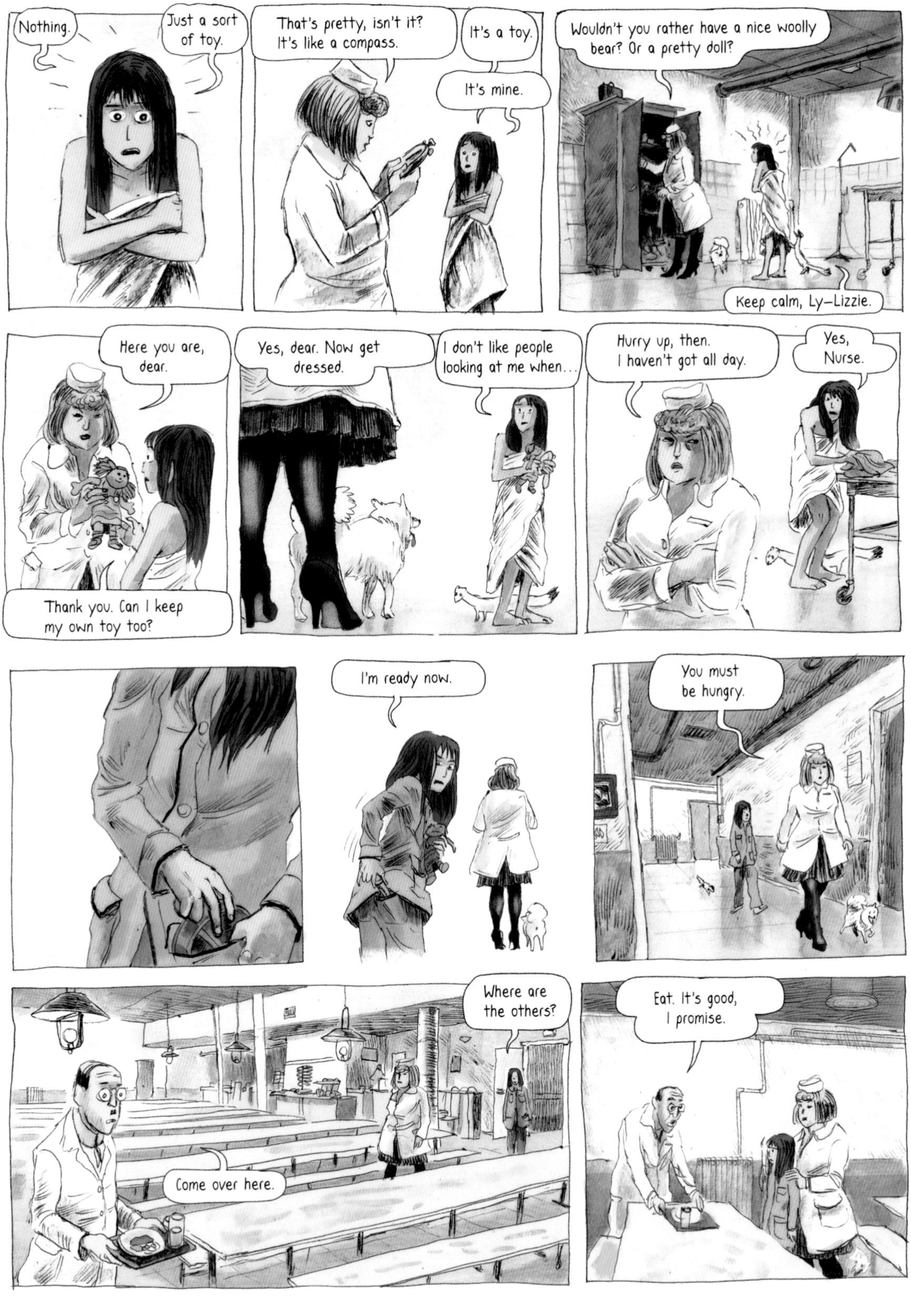
Nothing.
Just a sort of toy.
That's pretty, isn't it? It's like a compass.
It's a toy.
It's mine.
Wouldn't you rather have a nice woolly bear? Or a pretty doll?
Keep calm, Ly–Lizzie.
Here you are, dear.
Thank you. Can I keep my own toy too?
Yes, dear. Now get dressed.
I don't like people looking at me when...
Hurry up, then. I haven't got all day.
Yes, Nurse.
I'm ready now.
You must be hungry.
Where are the others?
Come over here.
Eat. It's good, I promise.

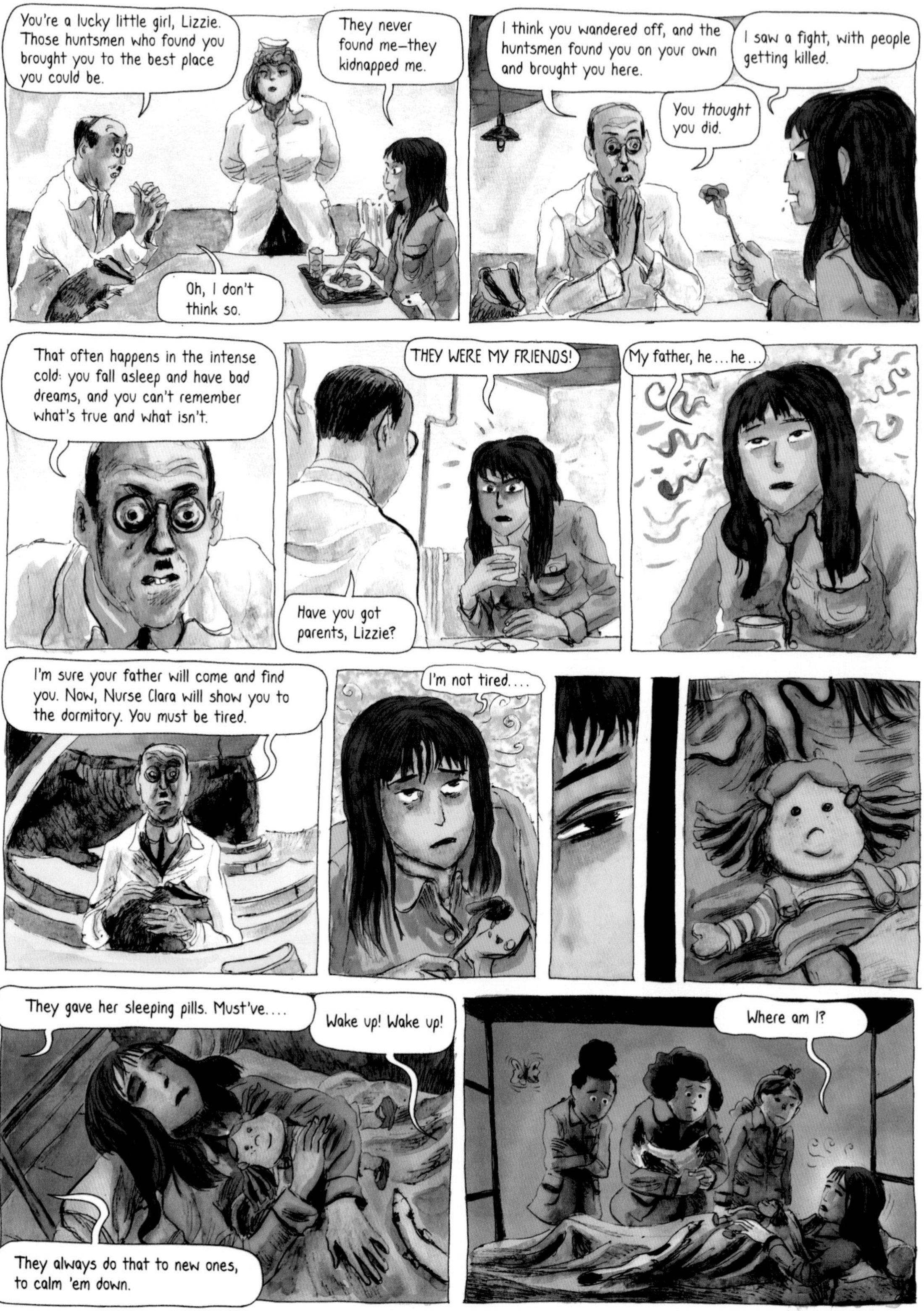
You're a lucky little girl, Lizzie. Those huntsmen who found you brought you to the best place you could be.
They never found me—they kidnapped me.
Oh, I don't think so.
I think you wandered off, and the huntsmen found you on your own and brought you here.
I saw a fight, with people getting killed.
You *thought* you did.
That often happens in the intense cold: you fall asleep and have bad dreams, and you can't remember what's true and what isn't.
THEY WERE MY FRIENDS!
Have you got parents, Lizzie?
My father, he...he...
I'm sure your father will come and find you. Now, Nurse Clara will show you to the dormitory. You must be tired.
I'm not tired....
They gave her sleeping pills. Must've....
Wake up! Wake up!
They always do that to new ones, to calm 'em down.
Where am I?

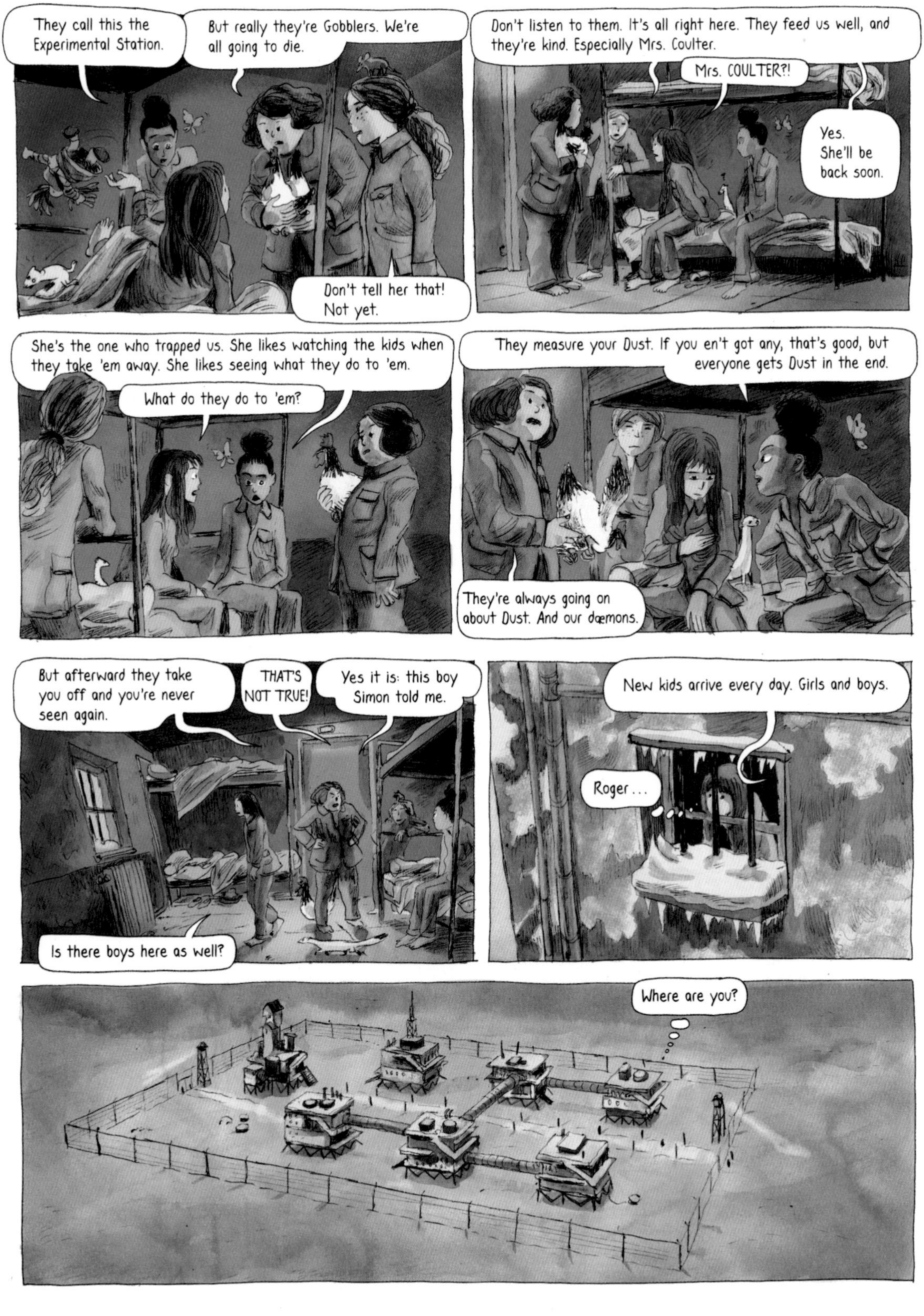
They call this the Experimental Station.
But really they're Gobblers. We're all going to die.
Don't tell her that! Not yet.
Don't listen to them. It's all right here. They feed us well, and they're kind. Especially Mrs. Coulter.
Mrs. COULTER?!
Yes. She'll be back soon.
She's the one who trapped us. She likes watching the kids when they take 'em away. She likes seeing what they do to 'em.
What do they do to 'em?
They measure your Dust. If you en't got any, that's good, but everyone gets Dust in the end.
They're always going on about Dust. And our dæmons.
But afterward they take you off and you're never seen again.
THAT'S NOT TRUE!
Yes it is: this boy Simon told me.
Is there boys here as well?
New kids arrive every day. Girls and boys.
Roger . . .
Where are you?

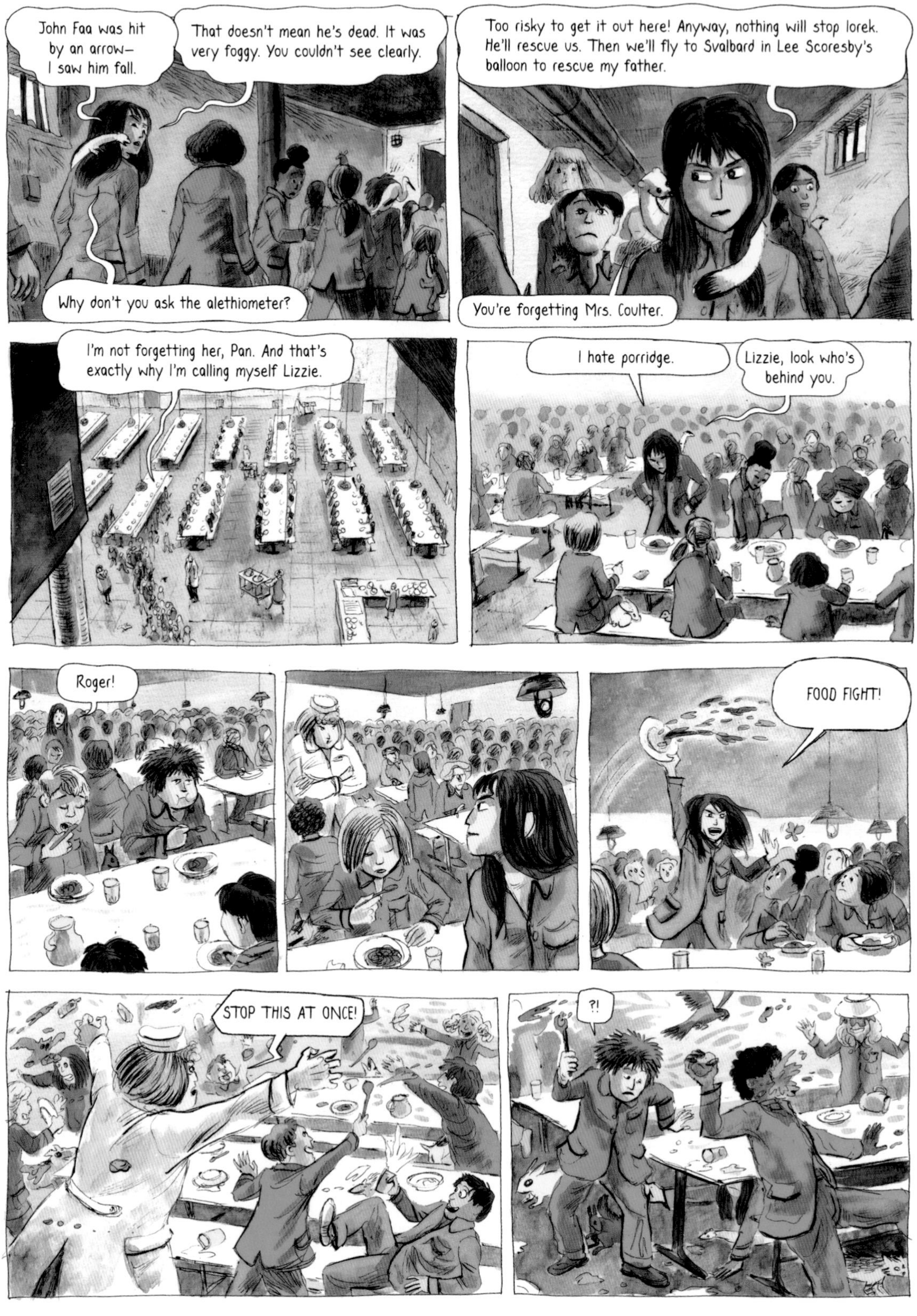

John Faa was hit by an arrow— I saw him fall.
That doesn't mean he's dead. It was very foggy. You couldn't see clearly.
Why don't you ask the alethiometer?
Too risky to get it out here! Anyway, nothing will stop Iorek. He'll rescue us. Then we'll fly to Svalbard in Lee Scoresby's balloon to rescue my father.
You're forgetting Mrs. Coulter.
I'm not forgetting her, Pan. And that's exactly why I'm calling myself Lizzie.
I hate porridge.
Lizzie, look who's behind you.
Roger!
FOOD FIGHT!
STOP THIS AT ONCE!
?!

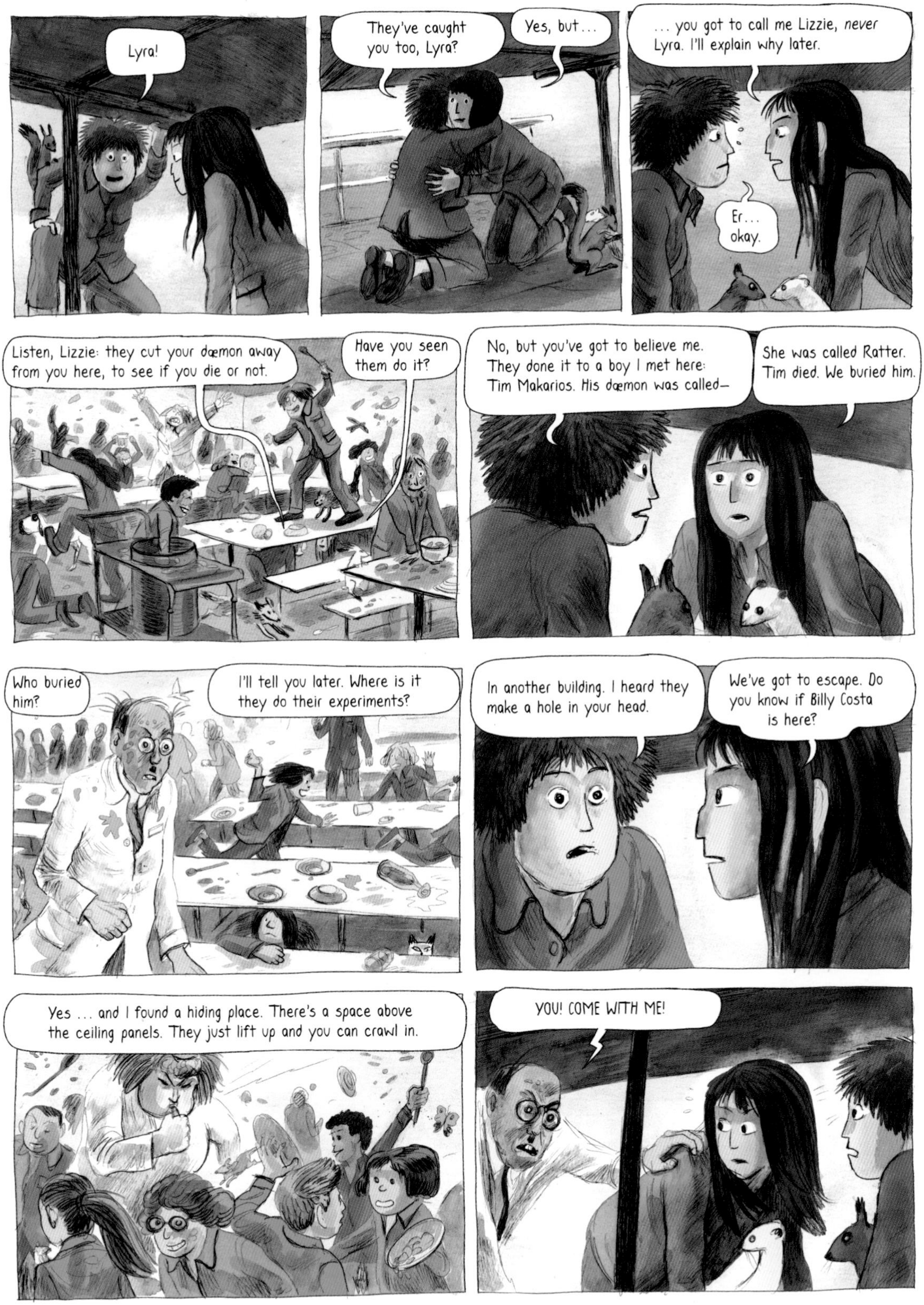
Lyra!
They've caught you too, Lyra?
Yes, but...
... you got to call me Lizzie, *never* Lyra. I'll explain why later.
Er... okay.
Listen, Lizzie: they cut your dæmon away from you here, to see if you die or not.
Have you seen them do it?
No, but you've got to believe me. They done it to a boy I met here: Tim Makarios. His dæmon was called—
She was called Ratter. Tim died. We buried him.
Who buried him?
I'll tell you later. Where is it they do their experiments?
In another building. I heard they make a hole in your head.
We've got to escape. Do you know if Billy Costa is here?
Yes ... and I found a hiding place. There's a space above the ceiling panels. They just lift up and you can crawl in.
YOU! COME WITH ME!

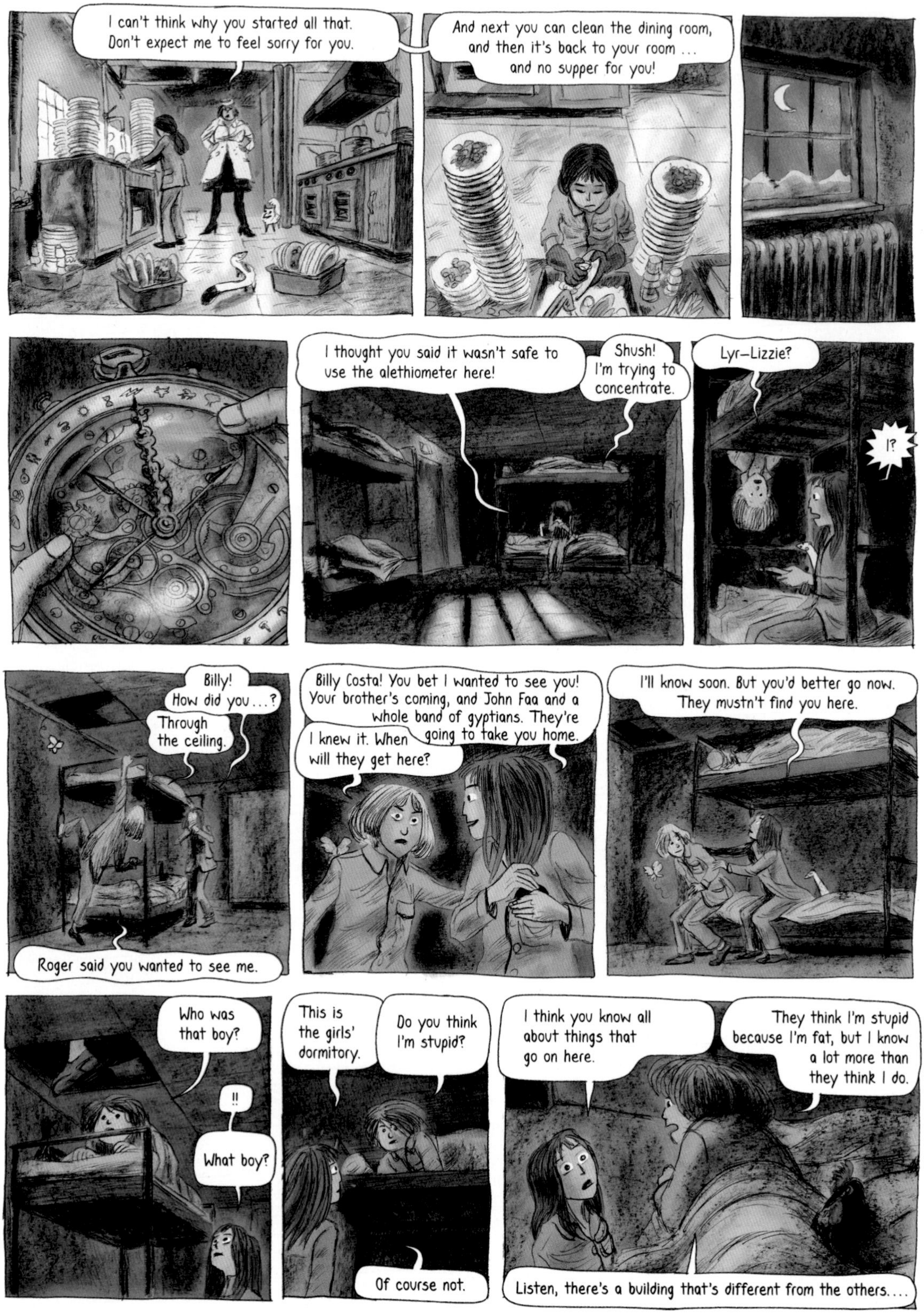
I can't think why you started all that. Don't expect me to feel sorry for you.
And next you can clean the dining room, and then it's back to your room . . . and no supper for you!
I thought you said it wasn't safe to use the alethiometer here!
Shush! I'm trying to concentrate.
Lyr—Lizzie?
!?
Billy! How did you . . . ?
Through the ceiling.
Roger said you wanted to see me.
Billy Costa! You bet I wanted to see you! Your brother's coming, and John Faa and a whole band of gyptians. They're going to take you home.
I knew it. When will they get here?
I'll know soon. But you'd better go now. They mustn't find you here.
Who was that boy?
!!
What boy?
This is the girls' dormitory.
Do you think I'm stupid?
Of course not.
I think you know all about things that go on here.
They think I'm stupid because I'm fat, but I know a lot more than they think I do.
Listen, there's a building that's different from the others. . . .

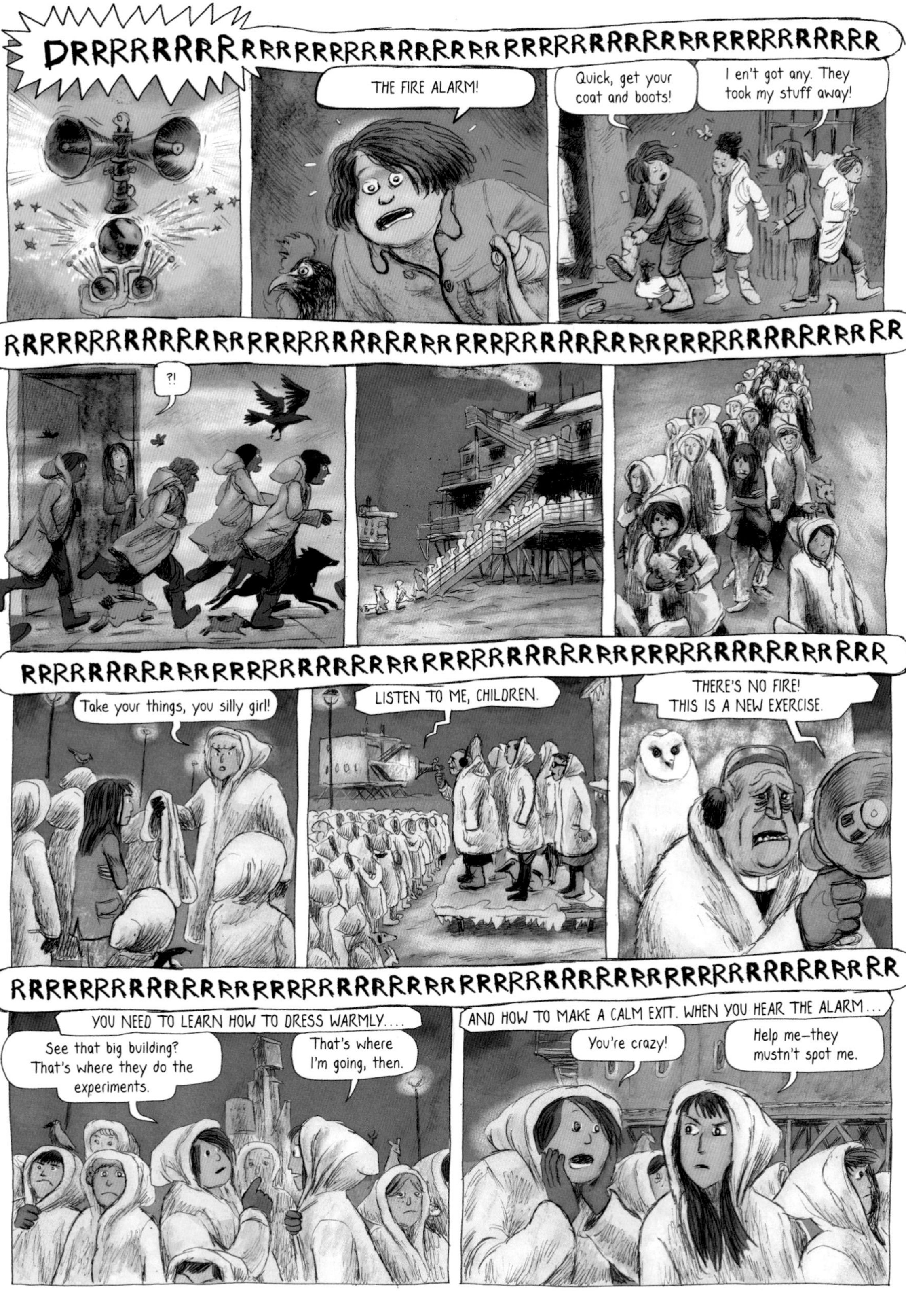
DRRRRRRRRRRRRRRRRRRRRRRRRRRRRRRRRRRRRRRRRRRRRRRR
THE FIRE ALARM!
Quick, get your coat and boots!
I en't got any. They took my stuff away!
RRRRRRRRRRRRRRRRRRRRRRRRRRRRRRRRRRRRRRRRRRRRRRRRRR
?!
RRRRRRRRRRRRRRRRRRRRRRRRRRRRRRRRRRRRRRRRRRRRRRRR
Take your things, you silly girl!
LISTEN TO ME, CHILDREN.
THERE'S NO FIRE! THIS IS A NEW EXERCISE.
RRRRRRRRRRRRRRRRRRRRRRRRRRRRRRRRRRRRRRRRRRRRRRRRRR
YOU NEED TO LEARN HOW TO DRESS WARMLY....
See that big building? That's where they do the experiments.
That's where I'm going, then.
AND HOW TO MAKE A CALM EXIT. WHEN YOU HEAR THE ALARM...
You're crazy!
Help me—they mustn't spot me.

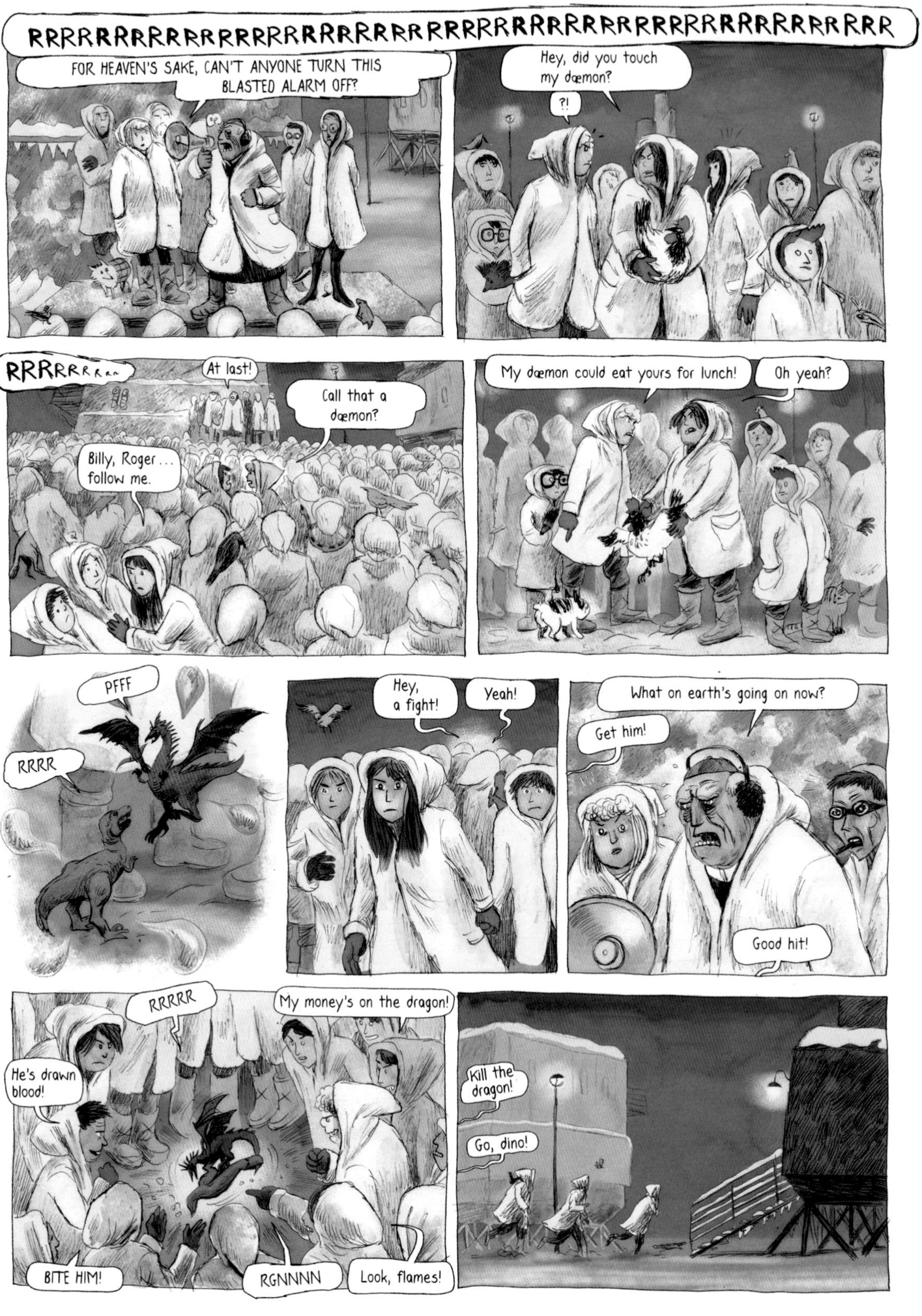
RRRRRRRRRRRRRRRRRRRRRRRRRRRRRRRRRRRRRRRRRR
FOR HEAVEN'S SAKE, CAN'T ANYONE TURN THIS BLASTED ALARM OFF?
Hey, did you touch my dæmon?
?!
RRRRRRRR
At last!
Call that a dæmon?
Billy, Roger... follow me.
My dæmon could eat yours for lunch!
Oh yeah?
PFFF
RRRR
Hey, a fight!
Yeah!
What on earth's going on now?
Get him!
Good hit!
RRRRR
My money's on the dragon!
He's drawn blood!
BITE HIM!
RGNNNN
Look, flames!
Kill the dragon!
Go, dino!

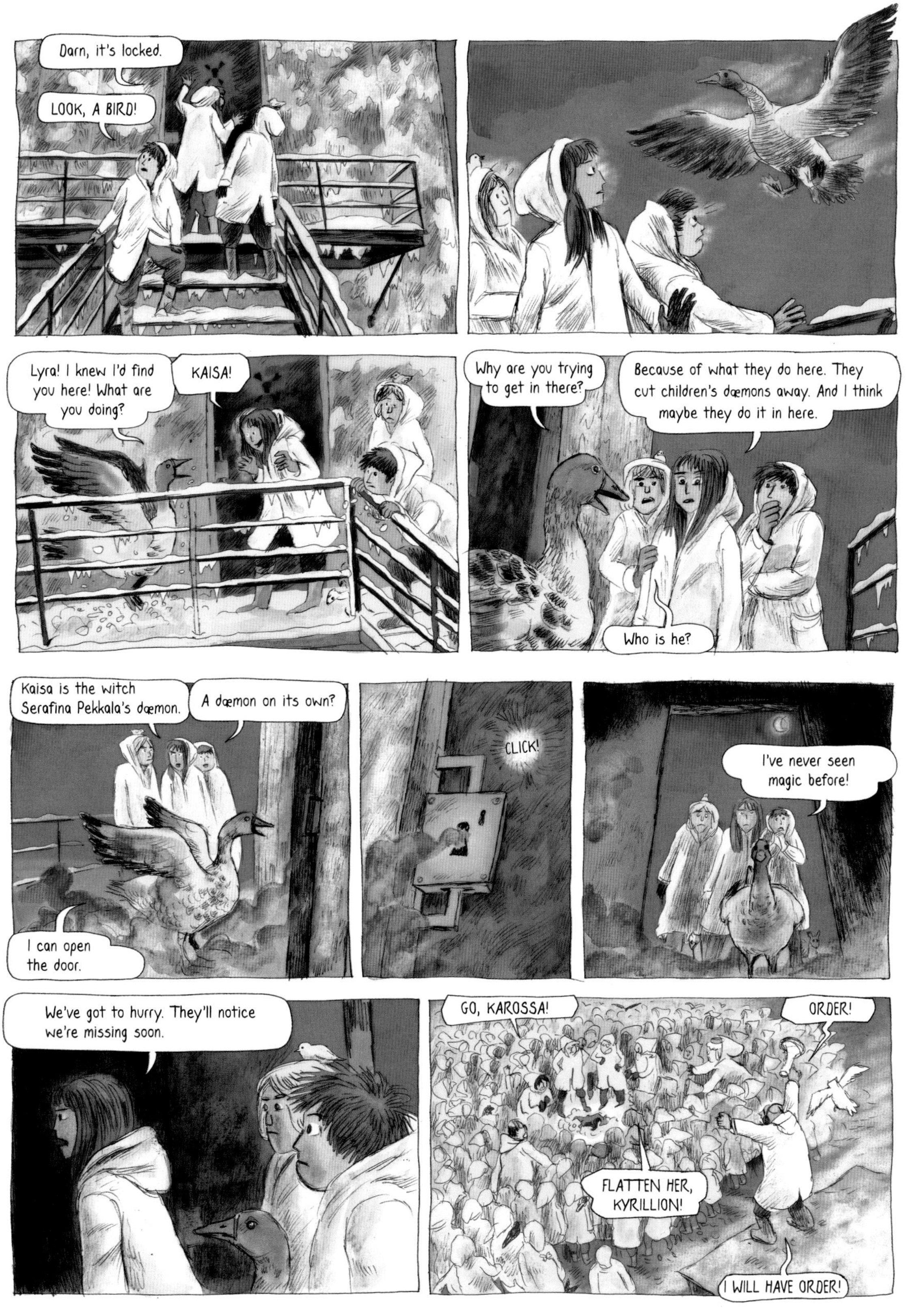
Darn, it's locked.
LOOK, A BIRD!
Lyra! I knew I'd find you here! What are you doing?
KAISA!
Why are you trying to get in there?
Because of what they do here. They cut children's dæmons away. And I think maybe they do it in here.
Who is he?
Kaisa is the witch Serafina Pekkala's dæmon.
A dæmon on its own?
I can open the door.
CLICK!
I've never seen magic before!
We've got to hurry. They'll notice we're missing soon.
GO, KAROSSA!
ORDER!
FLATTEN HER, KYRILLION!
I WILL HAVE ORDER!

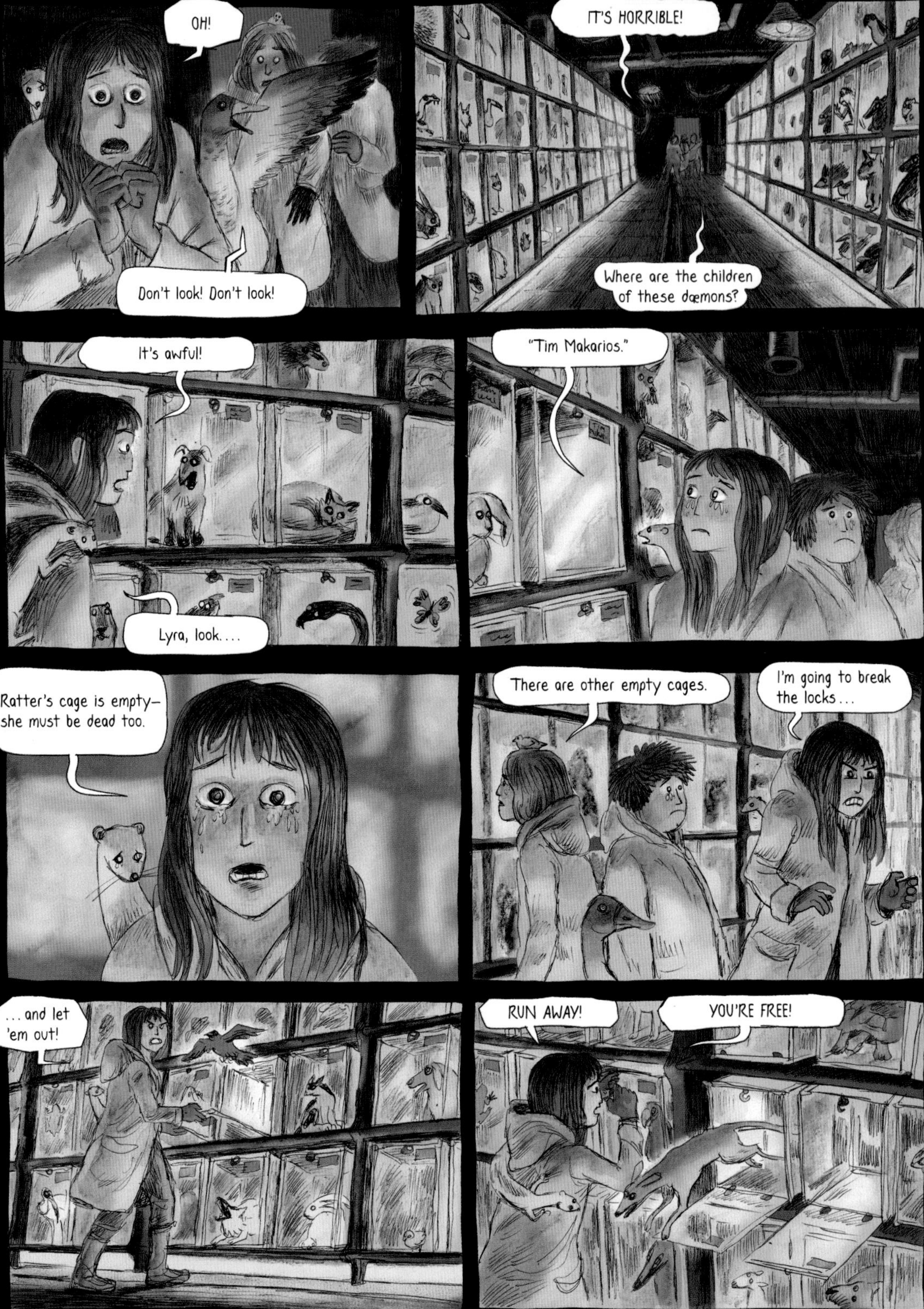
OH!
Don't look! Don't look!
IT'S HORRIBLE!
Where are the children of these dæmons?
It's awful!
Lyra, look. . . .
"Tim Makarios."
Ratter's cage is empty—she must be dead too.
There are other empty cages.
I'm going to break the locks . . .
. . . and let 'em out!
RUN AWAY!
YOU'RE FREE!

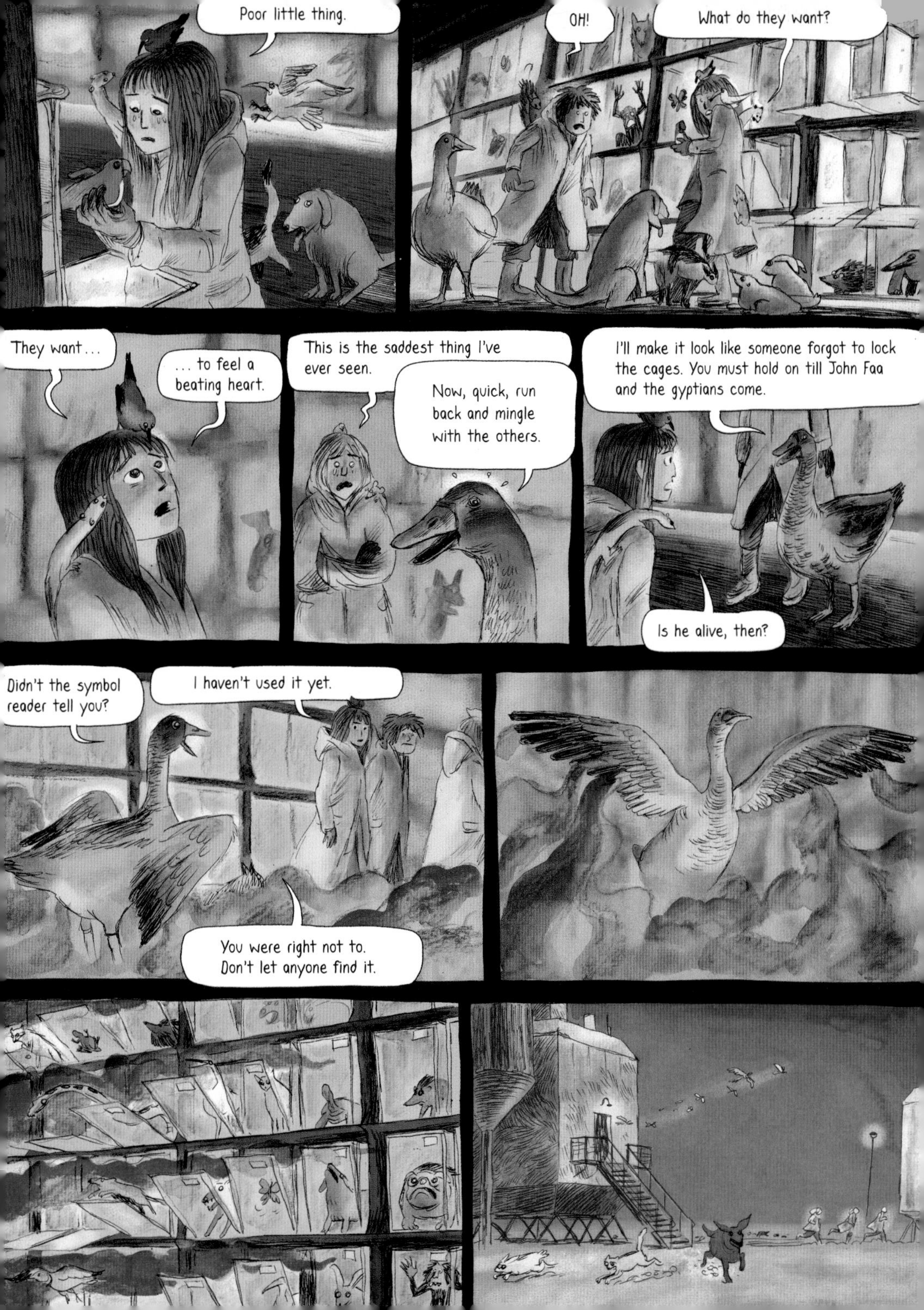

Poor little thing.
OH!
What do they want?
They want...
... to feel a beating heart.
This is the saddest thing I've ever seen.
Now, quick, run back and mingle with the others.
I'll make it look like someone forgot to lock the cages. You must hold on till John Faa and the gyptians come.
Is he alive, then?
Didn't the symbol reader tell you?
I haven't used it yet.
You were right not to. Don't let anyone find it.

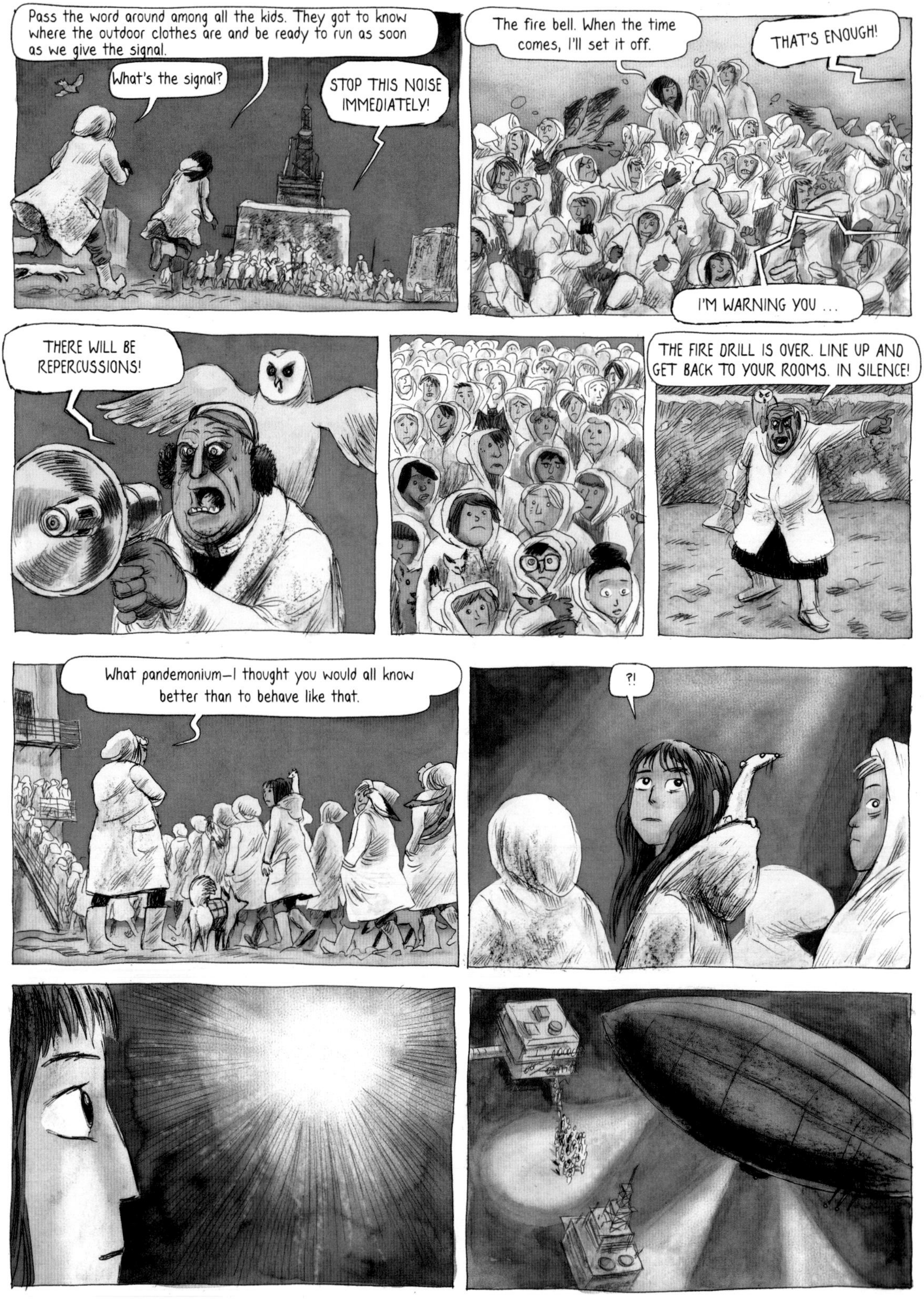
Pass the word around among all the kids. They got to know where the outdoor clothes are and be ready to run as soon as we give the signal.
What's the signal?
STOP THIS NOISE IMMEDIATELY!
The fire bell. When the time comes, I'll set it off.
THAT'S ENOUGH!
I'M WARNING YOU . . .
THERE WILL BE REPERCUSSIONS!
THE FIRE DRILL IS OVER. LINE UP AND GET BACK TO YOUR ROOMS. IN SILENCE!
What pandemonium—I thought you would all know better than to behave like that.
?!

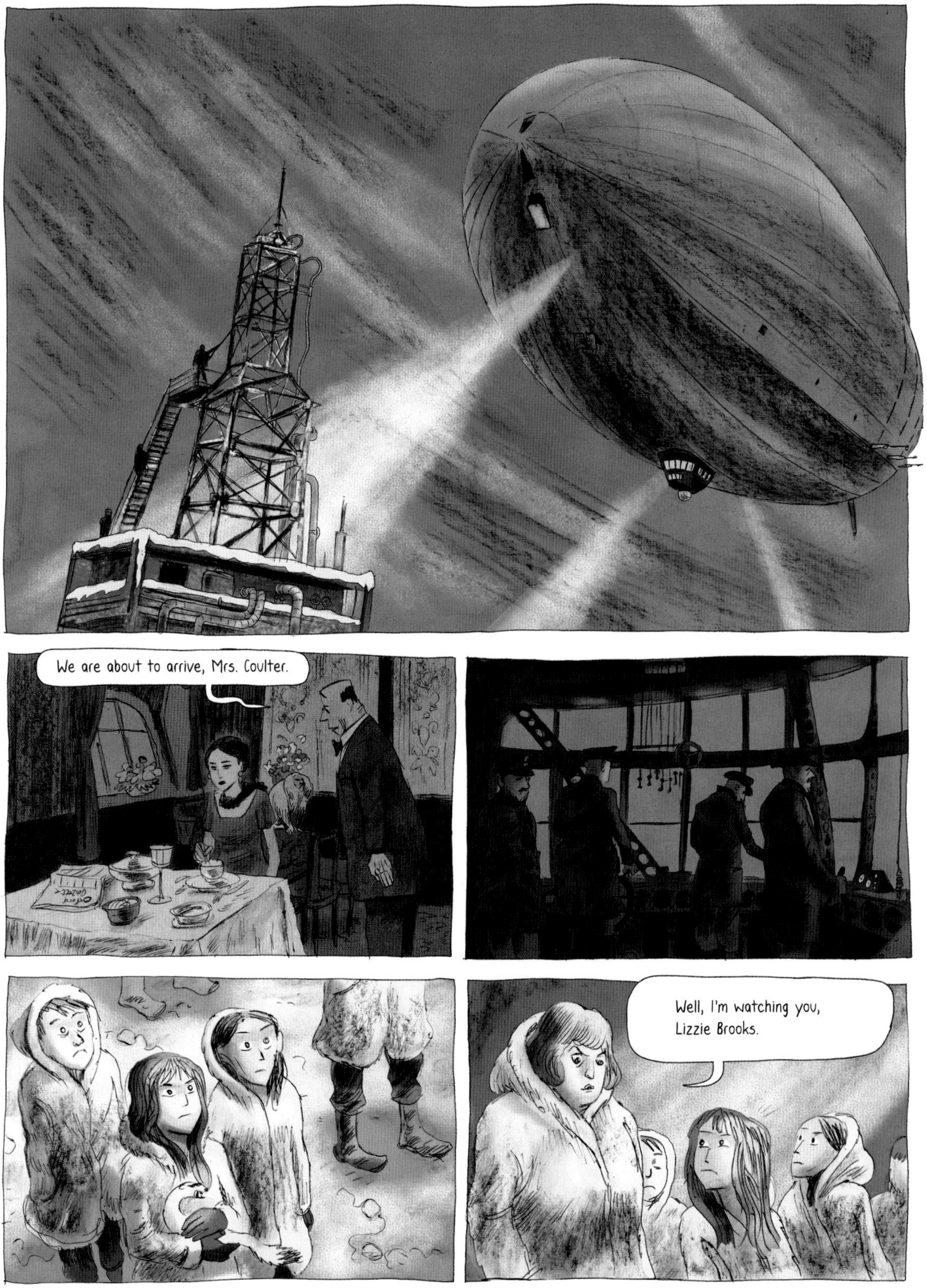
We are about to arrive, Mrs. Coulter.
Well, I'm watching you, Lizzie Brooks.

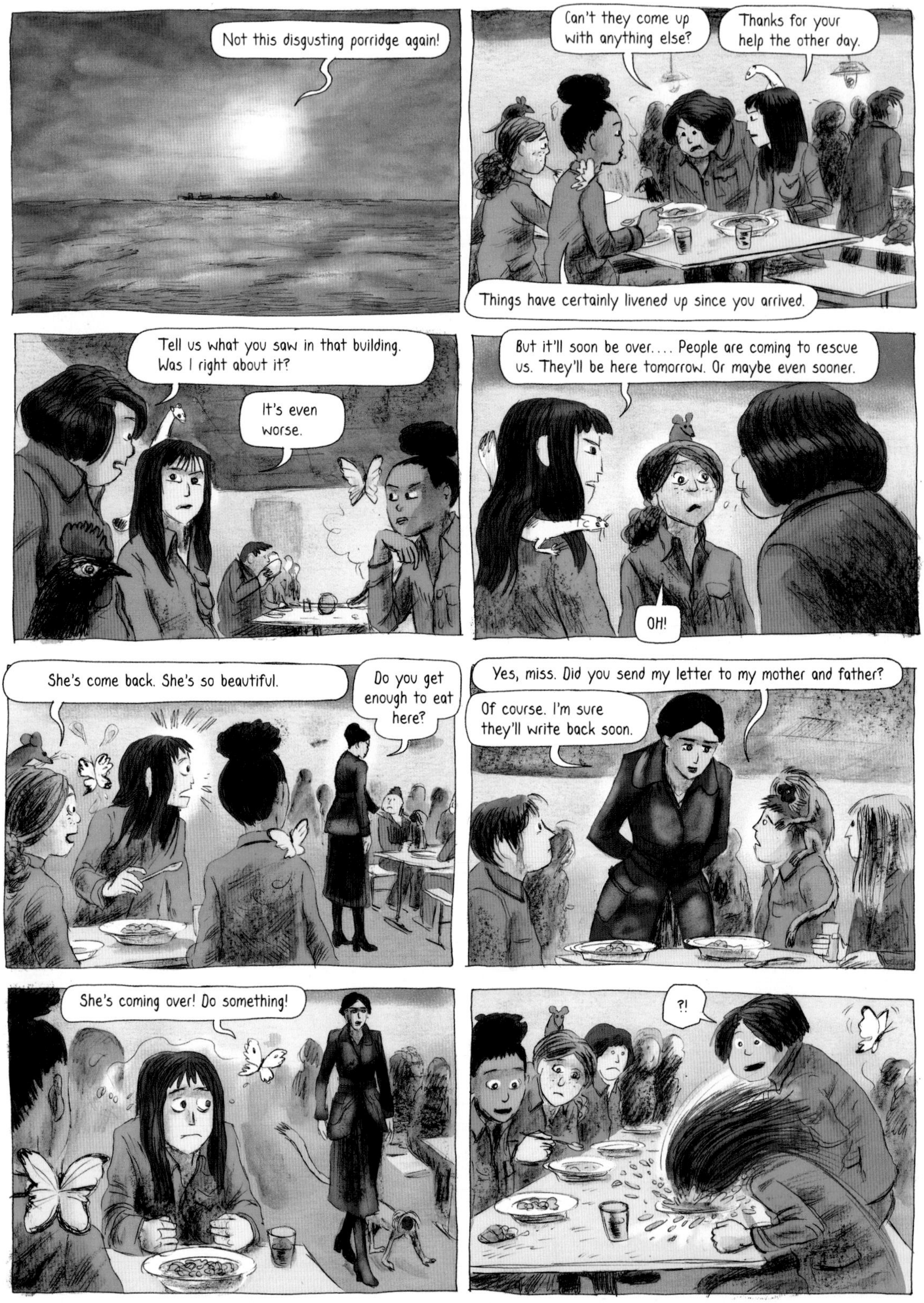
Not this disgusting porridge again!
Can't they come up with anything else?
Thanks for your help the other day.
Things have certainly livened up since you arrived.
Tell us what you saw in that building. Was I right about it?
It's even worse.
But it'll soon be over.... People are coming to rescue us. They'll be here tomorrow. Or maybe even sooner.
OH!
She's come back. She's so beautiful.
Do you get enough to eat here?
Yes, miss. Did you send my letter to my mother and father?
Of course. I'm sure they'll write back soon.
She's coming over! Do something!
?!

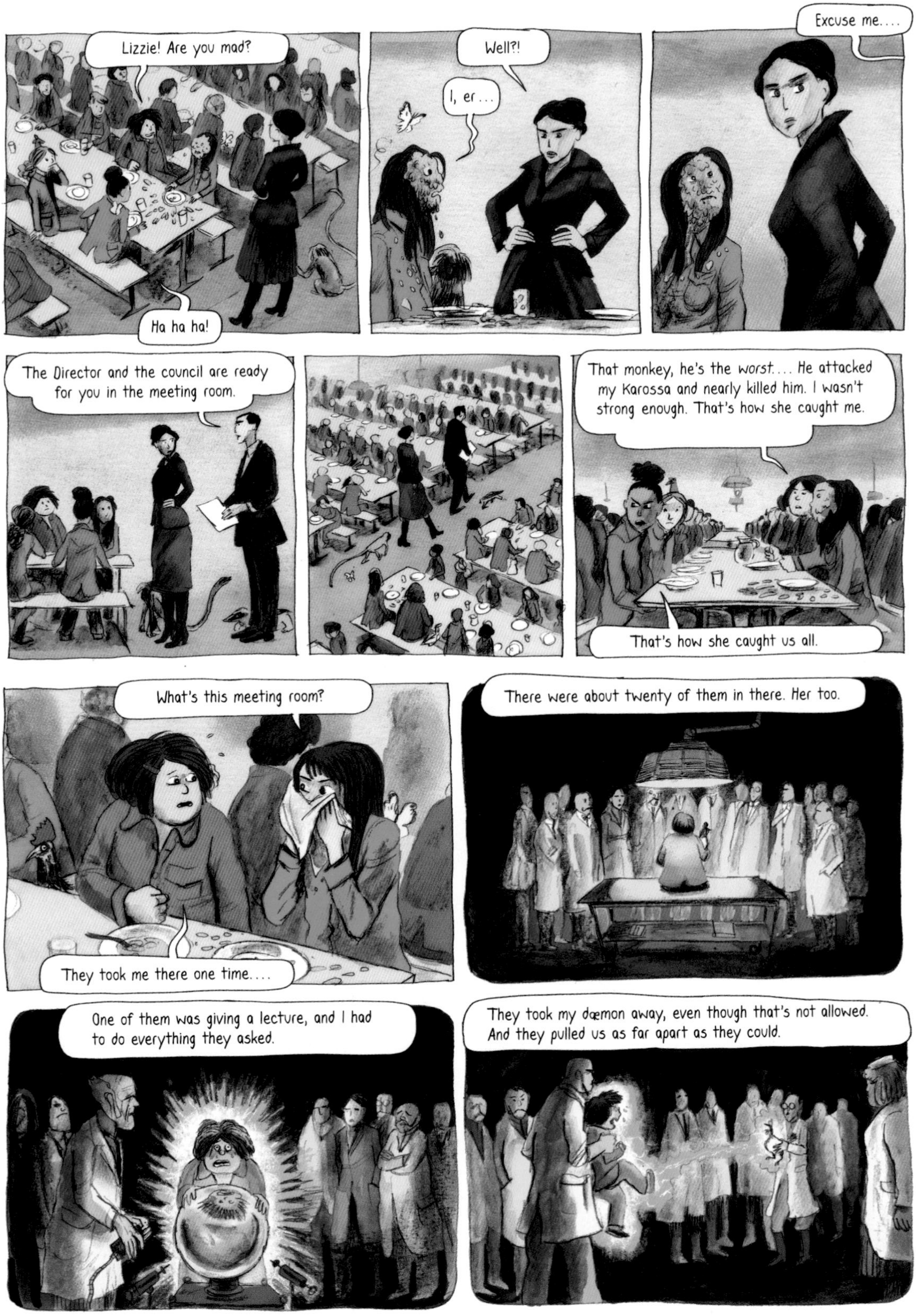
Lizzie! Are you mad?
Ha ha ha!
Well?!
I, er...
Excuse me....
The Director and the council are ready for you in the meeting room.
That monkey, he's the *worst*.... He attacked my Karossa and nearly killed him. I wasn't strong enough. That's how she caught me.
That's how she caught us all.
What's this meeting room?
They took me there one time....
There were about twenty of them in there. Her too.
One of them was giving a lecture, and I had to do everything they asked.
They took my dæmon away, even though that's not allowed. And they pulled us as far apart as they could.

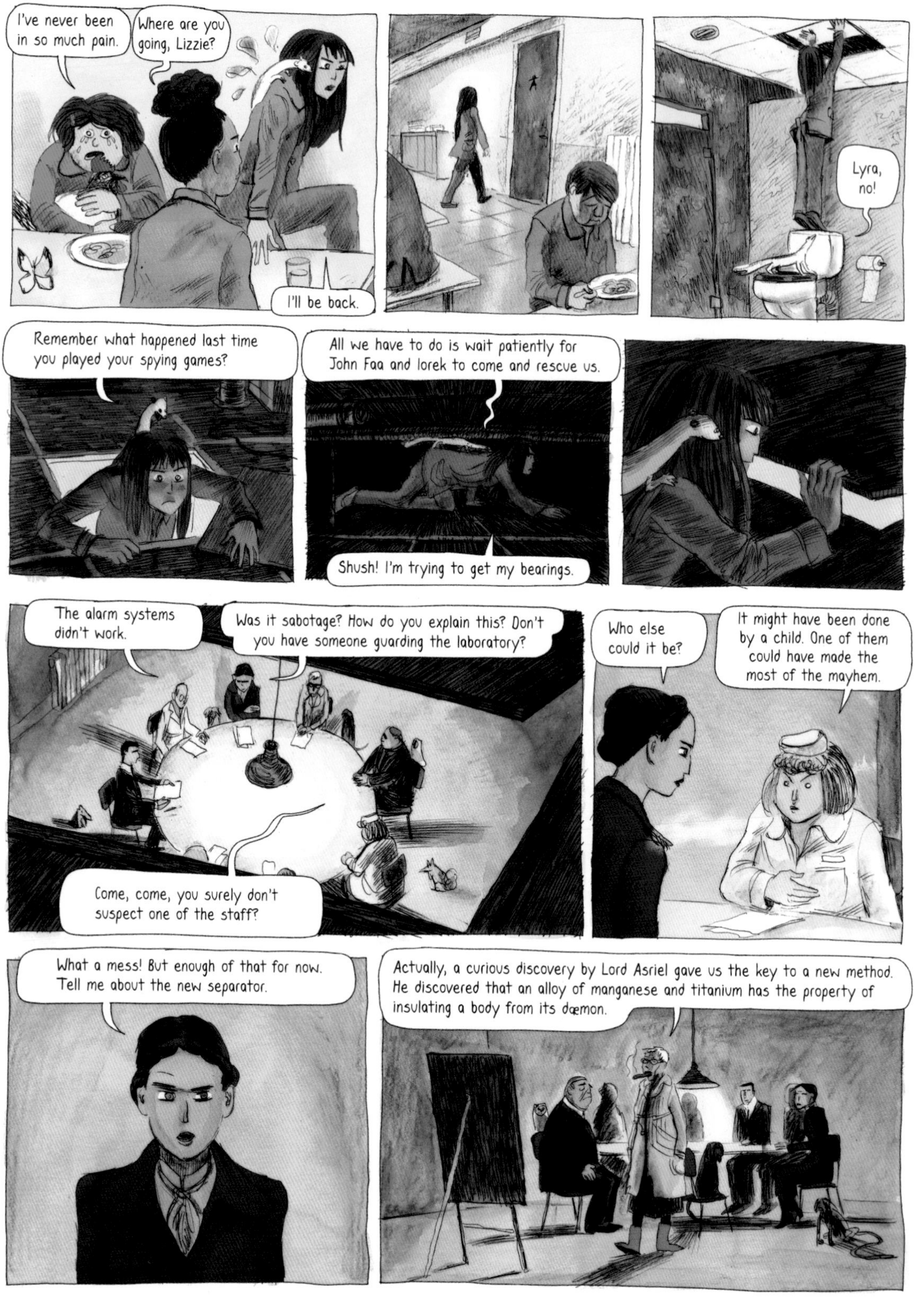
I've never been in so much pain.
Where are you going, Lizzie?
I'll be back.
Lyra, no!
Remember what happened last time you played your spying games?
All we have to do is wait patiently for John Faa and Iorek to come and rescue us.
Shush! I'm trying to get my bearings.
The alarm systems didn't work.
Was it sabotage? How do you explain this? Don't you have someone guarding the laboratory?
Come, come, you surely don't suspect one of the staff?
Who else could it be?
It might have been done by a child. One of them could have made the most of the mayhem.
What a mess! But enough of that for now. Tell me about the new separator.
Actually, a curious discovery by Lord Asriel gave us the key to a new method. He discovered that an alloy of manganese and titanium has the property of insulating a body from its dæmon.

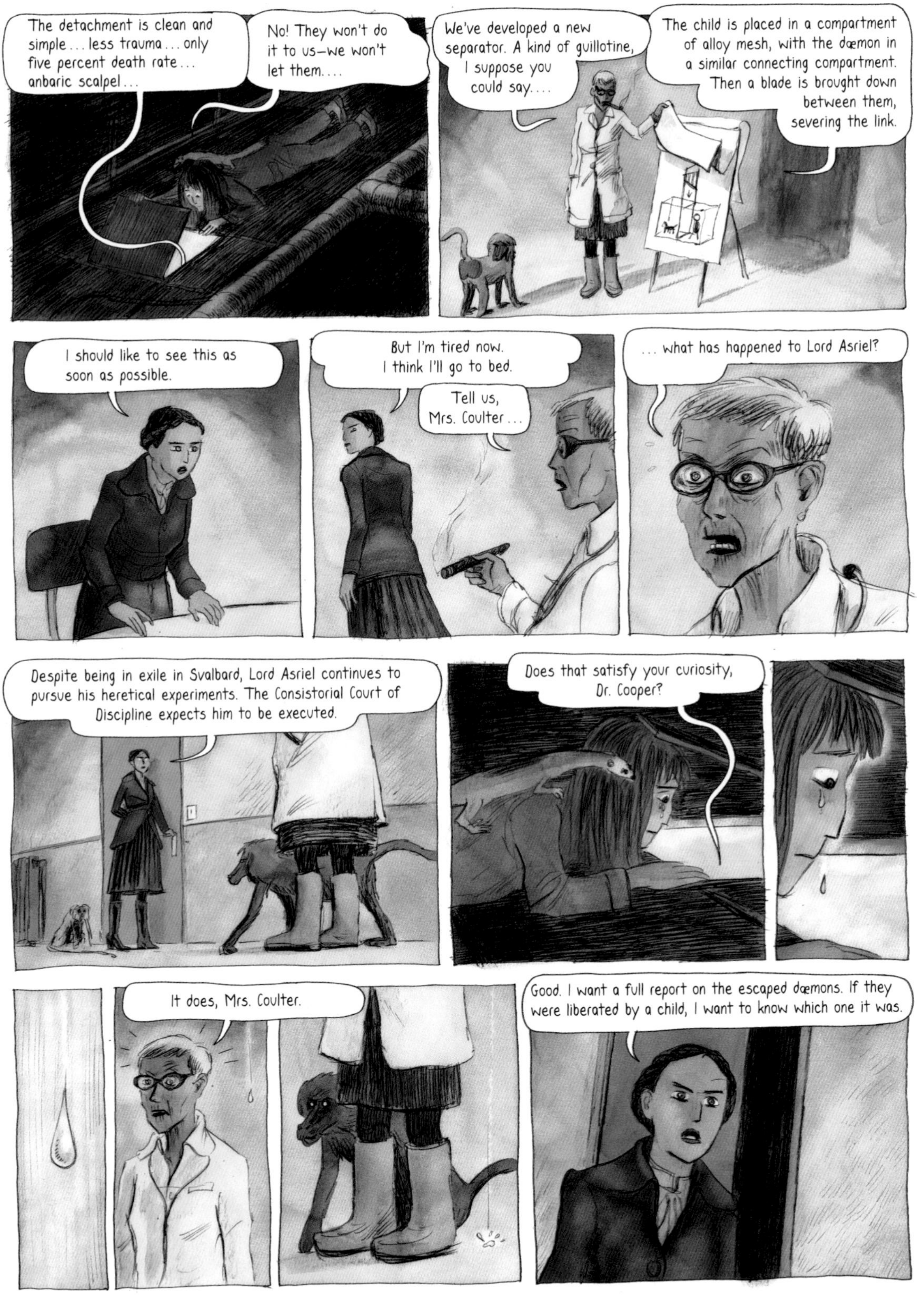
The detachment is clean and simple . . . less trauma . . . only five percent death rate . . . anbaric scalpel . . .
No! They won't do it to us—we won't let them. . . .
We've developed a new separator. A kind of guillotine, I suppose you could say. . . .
The child is placed in a compartment of alloy mesh, with the dæmon in a similar connecting compartment. Then a blade is brought down between them, severing the link.
I should like to see this as soon as possible.
But I'm tired now. I think I'll go to bed.
Tell us, Mrs. Coulter . . .
. . . what has happened to Lord Asriel?
Despite being in exile in Svalbard, Lord Asriel continues to pursue his heretical experiments. The Consistorial Court of Discipline expects him to be executed.
Does that satisfy your curiosity, Dr. Cooper?
It does, Mrs. Coulter.
Good. I want a full report on the escaped dæmons. If they were liberated by a child, I want to know which one it was.

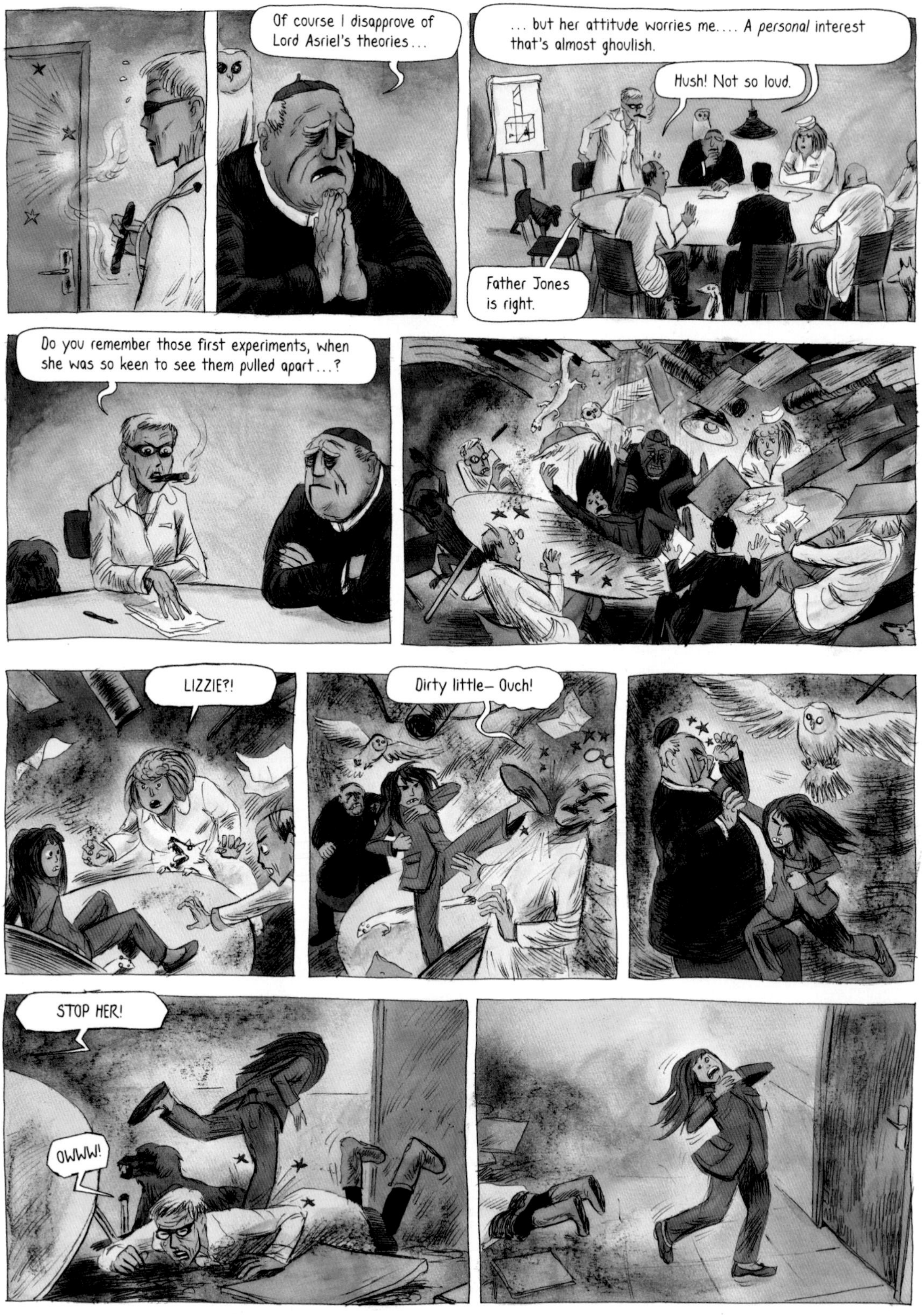
Of course I disapprove of Lord Asriel's theories...
... but her attitude worries me.... A *personal* interest that's almost ghoulish.
Hush! Not so loud.
Father Jones is right.
Do you remember those first experiments, when she was so keen to see them pulled apart...?
LIZZIE?!
Dirty little– Ouch!
STOP HER!
OWWW!

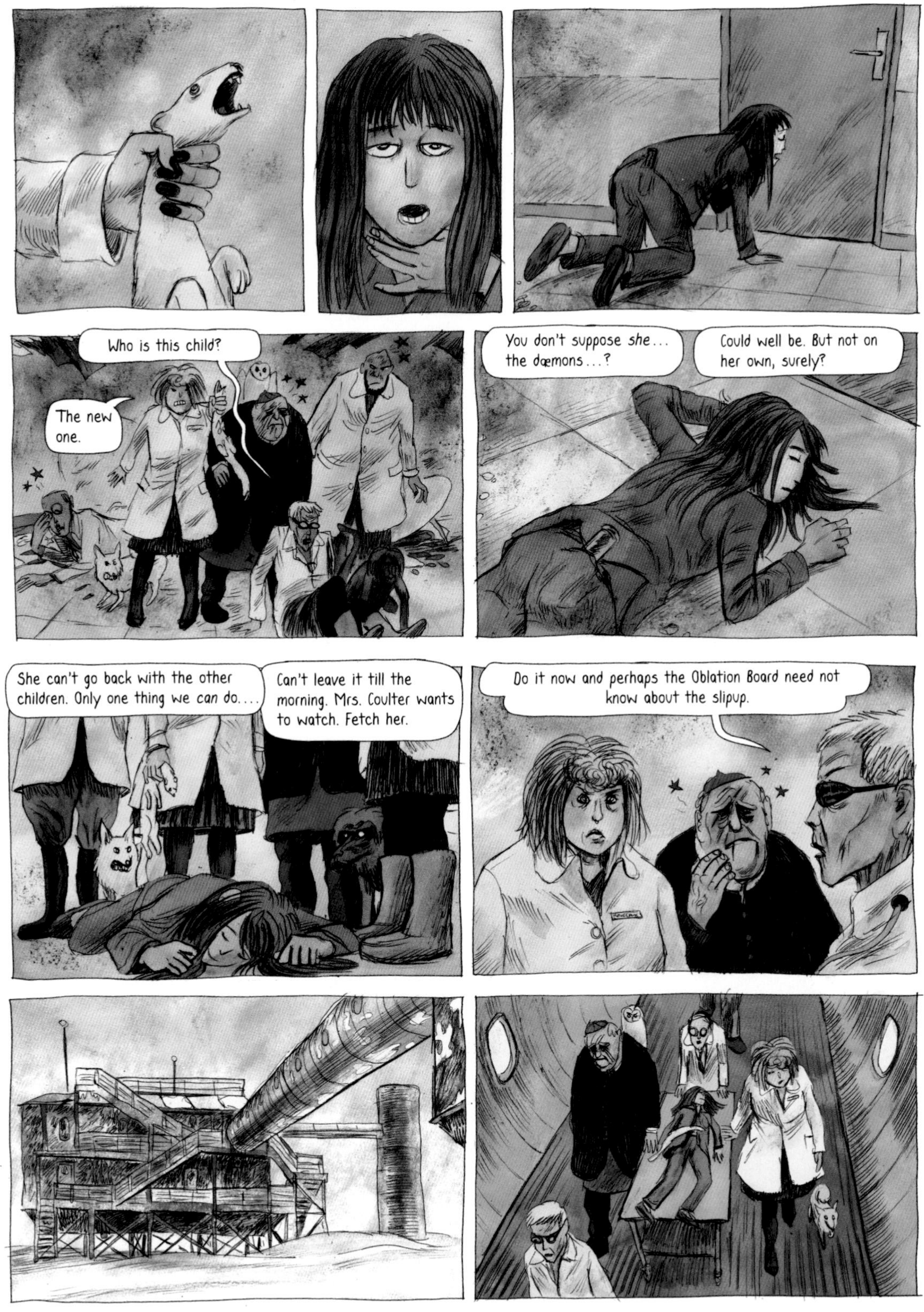
Who is this child?
The new one.
You don't suppose *she* . . . the dæmons . . . ?
Could well be. But not on her own, surely?
She can't go back with the other children. Only one thing we *can* do. . . .
Can't leave it till the morning. Mrs. Coulter wants to watch. Fetch her.
Do it now and perhaps the Oblation Board need not know about the slipup.

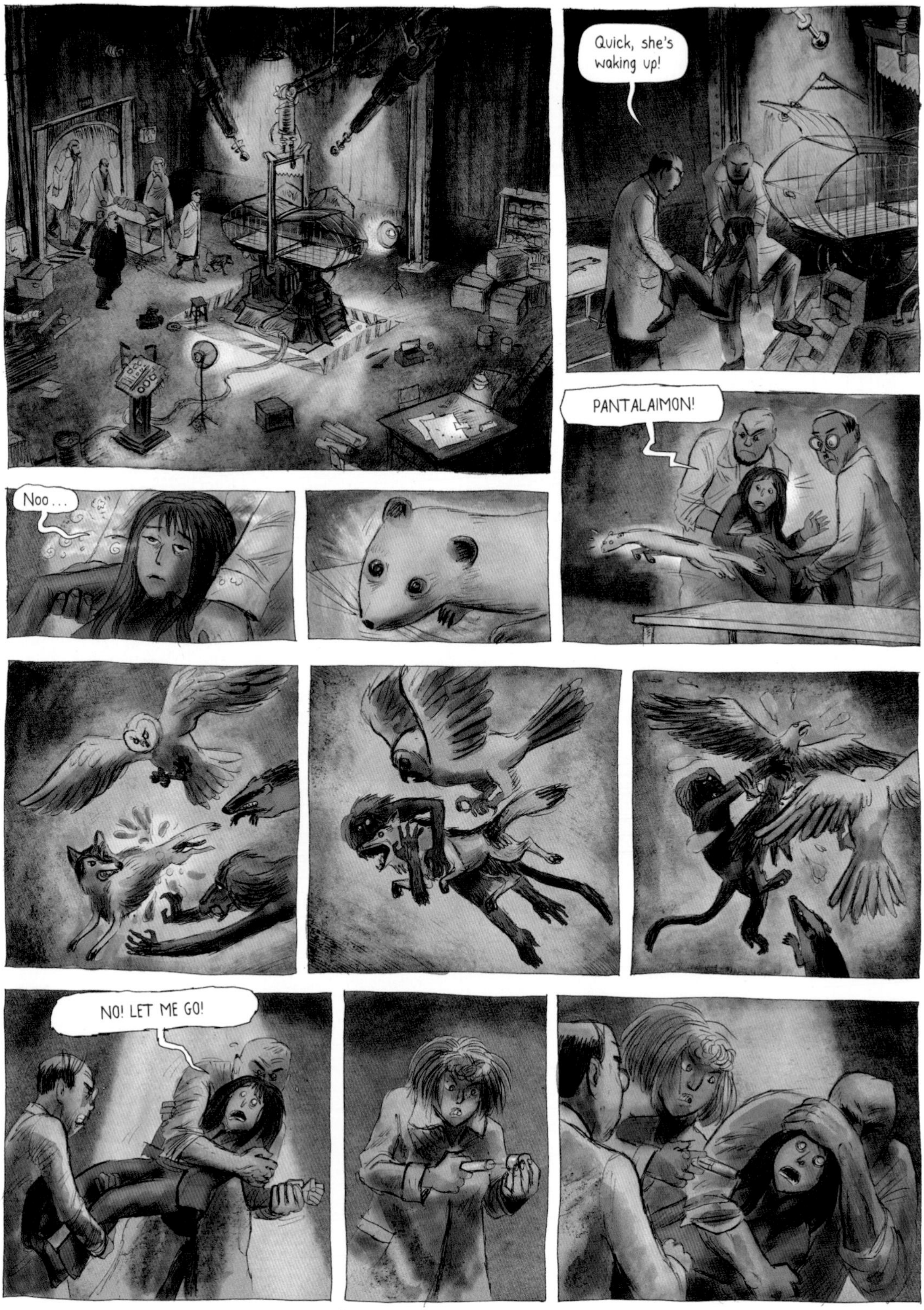
Quick, she's waking up!
PANTALAIMON!
Noo...
NO! LET ME GO!

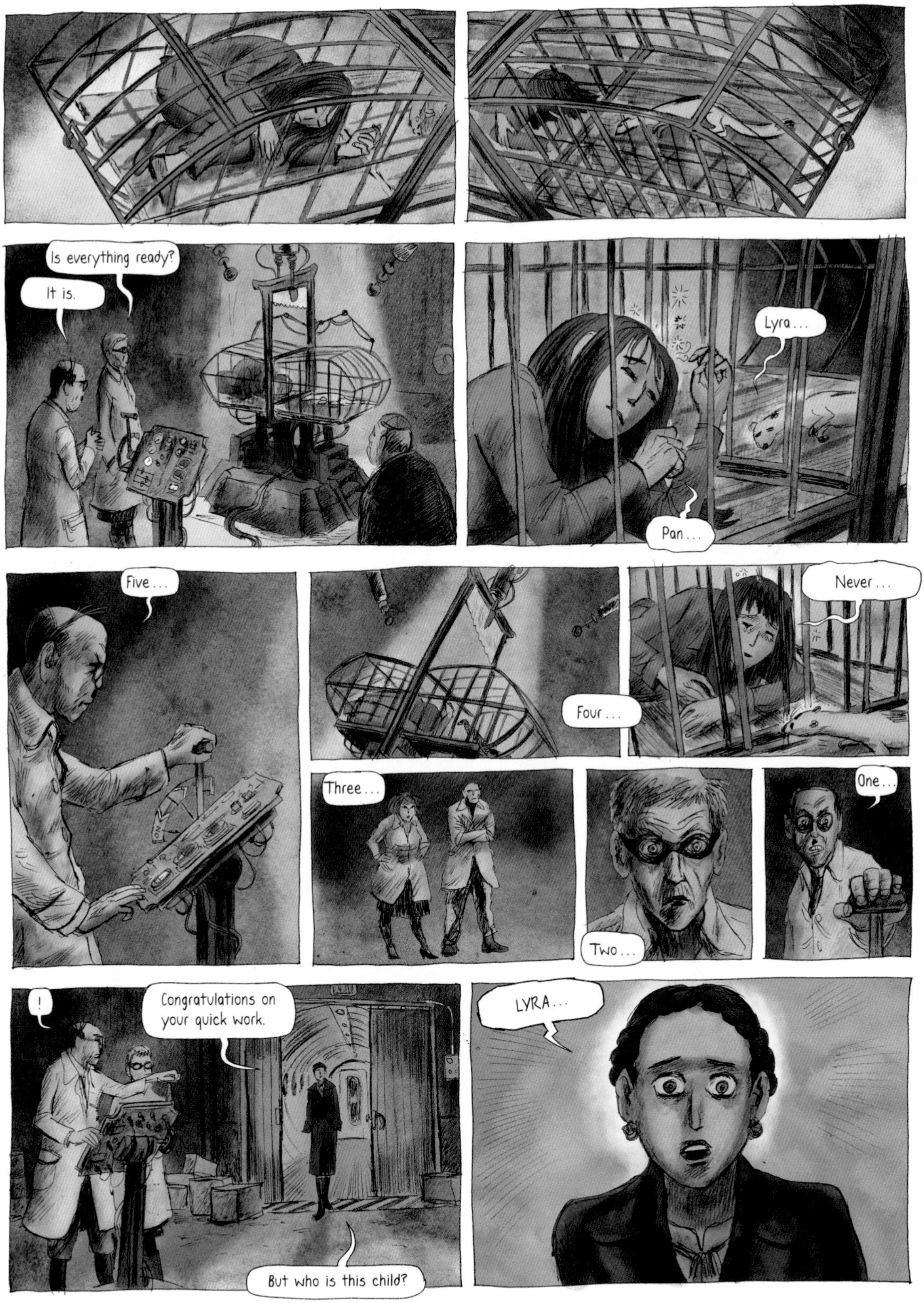
Is everything ready?
It is.
Lyra...
Pan...
Five...
Never...
Four...
Three...
Two...
One...
!
Congratulations on your quick work.
But who is this child?
LYRA...

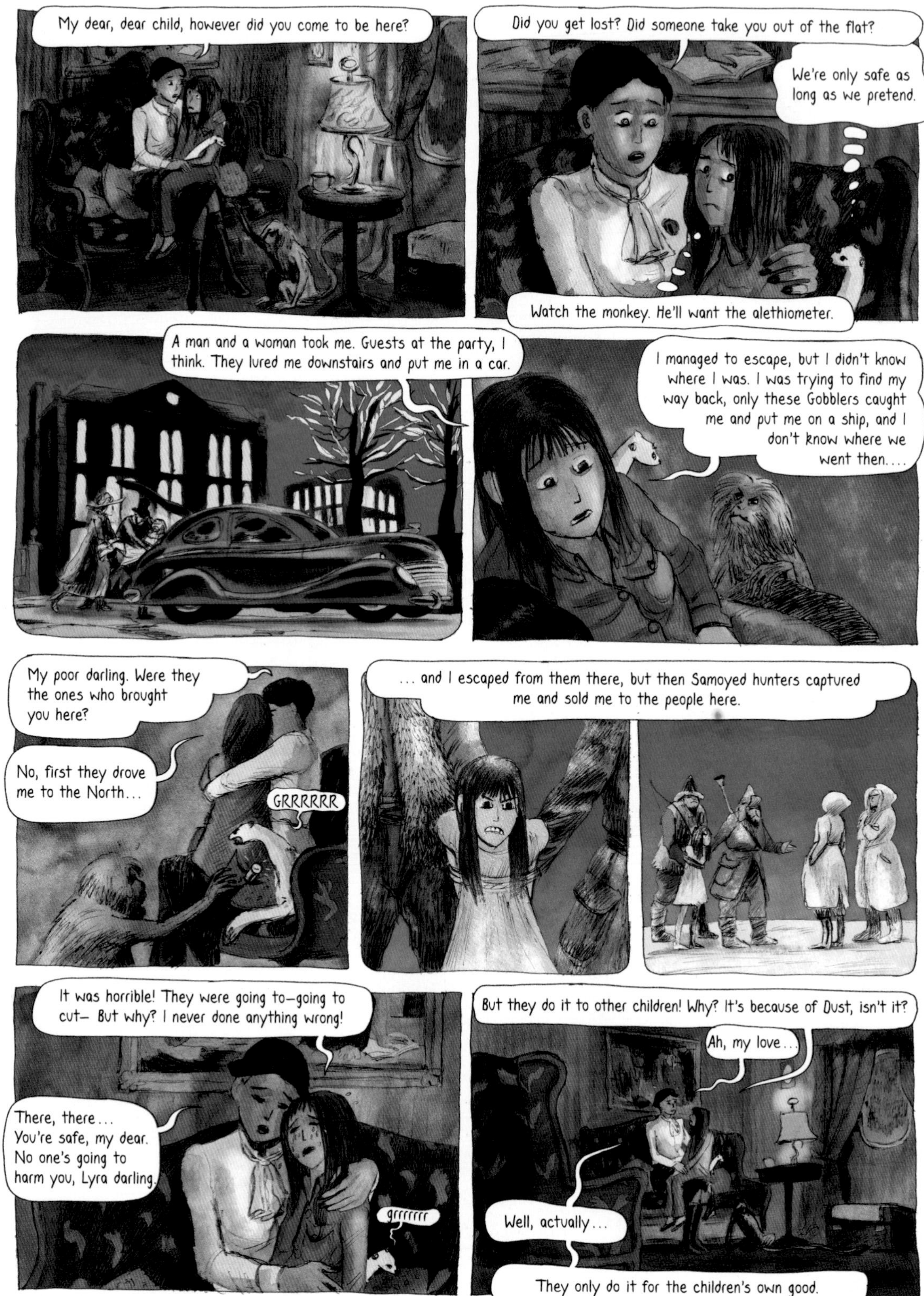
My dear, dear child, however did you come to be here?
Did you get lost? Did someone take you out of the flat?
We're only safe as long as we pretend.
Watch the monkey. He'll want the alethiometer.
A man and a woman took me. Guests at the party, I think. They lured me downstairs and put me in a car.
I managed to escape, but I didn't know where I was. I was trying to find my way back, only these Gobblers caught me and put me on a ship, and I don't know where we went then. . . .
My poor darling. Were they the ones who brought you here?
No, first they drove me to the North . . .
GRRRRRR
. . . and I escaped from them there, but then Samoyed hunters captured me and sold me to the people here.
It was horrible! They were going to—going to cut— But why? I never done anything wrong!
There, there . . . You're safe, my dear. No one's going to harm you, Lyra darling.
grrrrrrr
But they do it to other children! Why? It's because of Dust, isn't it?
Ah, my love . . .
Well, actually . . .
They only do it for the children's own good.

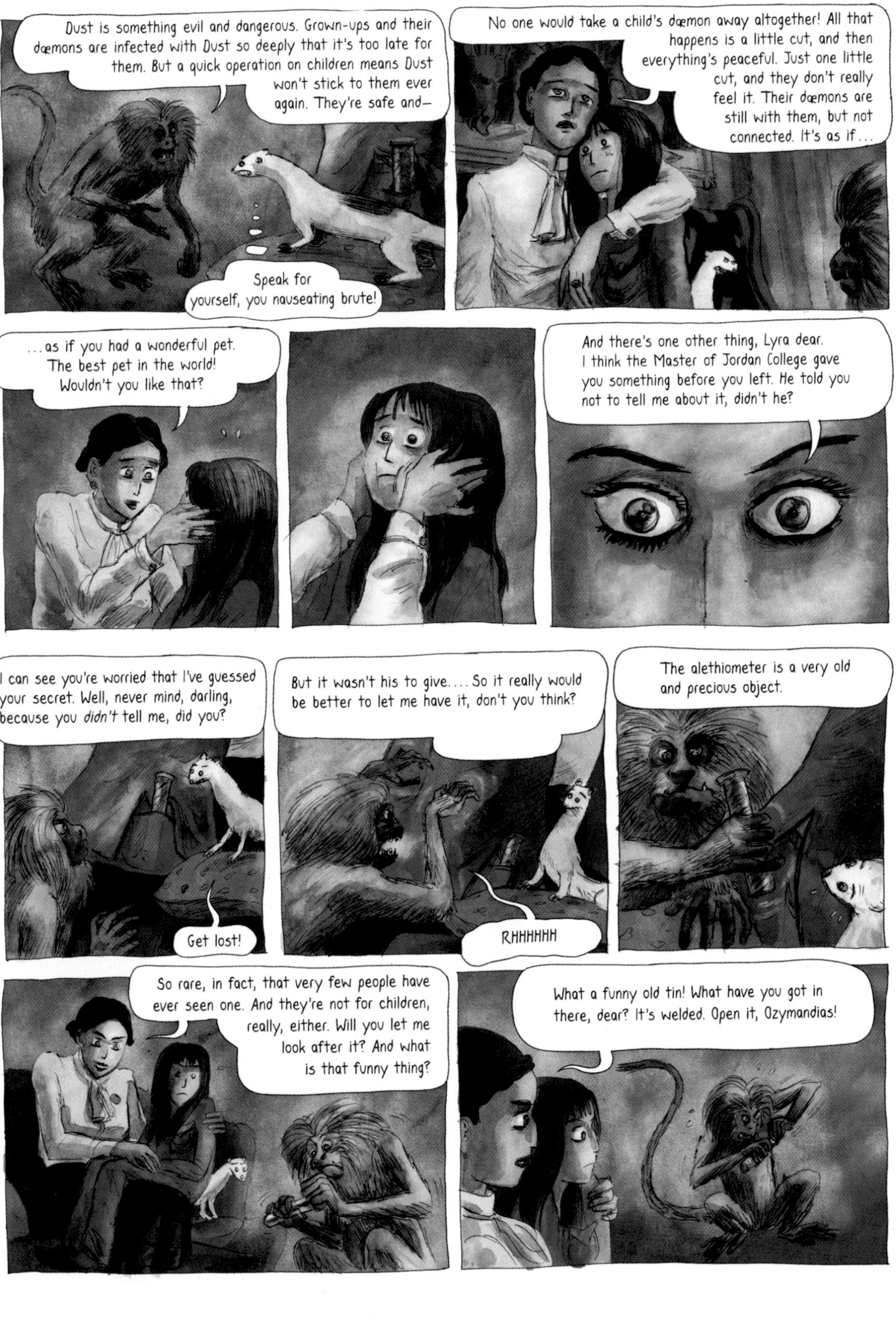
Dust is something evil and dangerous. Grown-ups and their dæmons are infected with Dust so deeply that it's too late for them. But a quick operation on children means Dust won't stick to them ever again. They're safe and—
Speak for yourself, you nauseating brute!
No one would take a child's dæmon away altogether! All that happens is a little cut, and then everything's peaceful. Just one little cut, and they don't really feel it. Their dæmons are still with them, but not connected. It's as if . . .
. . . as if you had a wonderful pet. The best pet in the world! Wouldn't you like that?
And there's one other thing, Lyra dear. I think the Master of Jordan College gave you something before you left. He told you not to tell me about it, didn't he?
I can see you're worried that I've guessed your secret. Well, never mind, darling, because you *didn't* tell me, did you?
Get lost!
But it wasn't his to give. . . . So it really would be better to let me have it, don't you think?
RHHHHHH
The alethiometer is a very old and precious object.
So rare, in fact, that very few people have ever seen one. And they're not for children, really, either. Will you let me look after it? And what is that funny thing?
What a funny old tin! What have you got in there, dear? It's welded. Open it, Ozymandias!

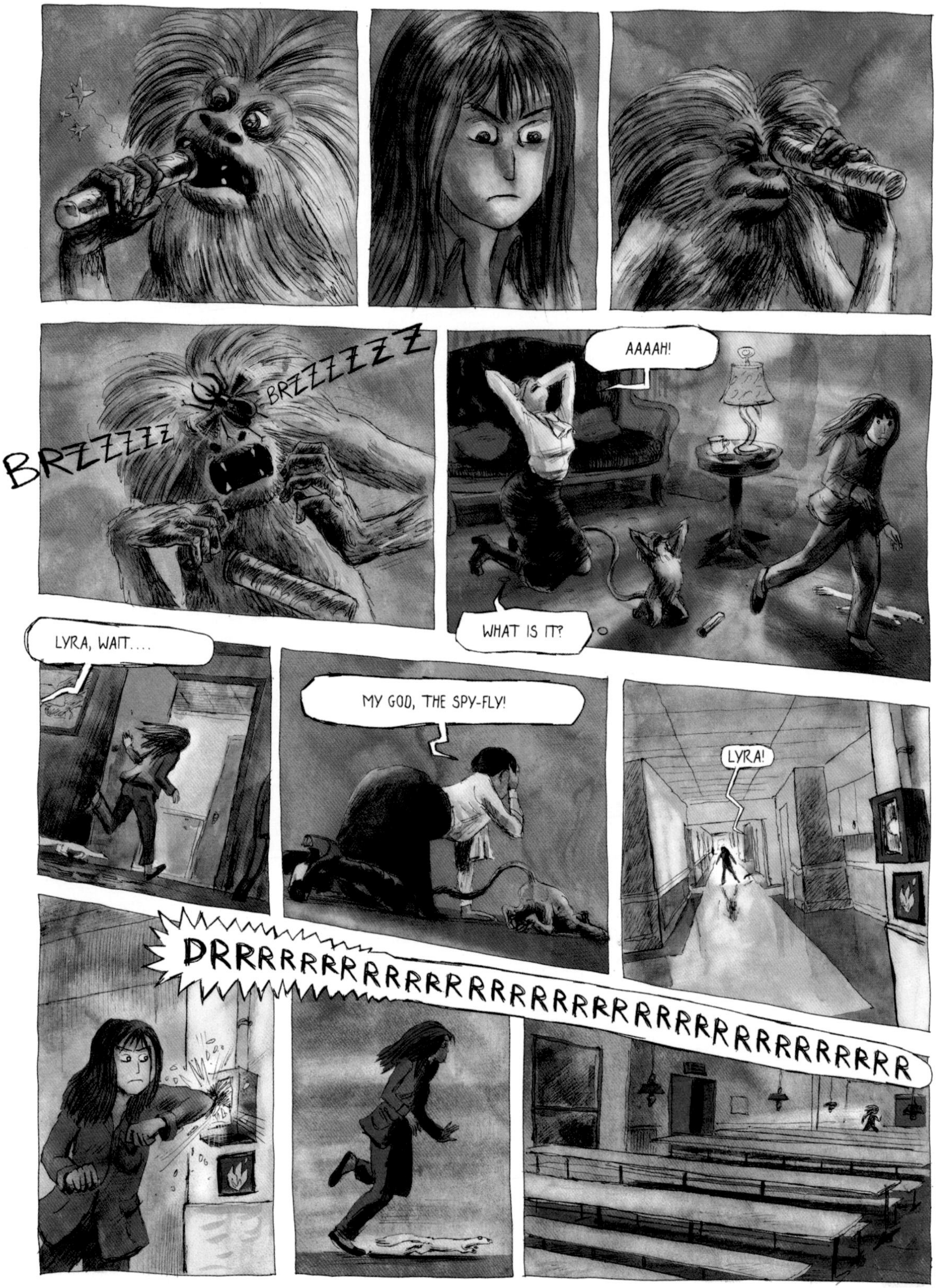
BRZZZZZZ
BRZZZZZZZZ
AAAAH!
WHAT IS IT?
LYRA, WAIT....
MY GOD, THE SPY-FLY!
LYRA!
DRRRRRRRRRRRRRRRRRRRRRRRRRRRRRRRR

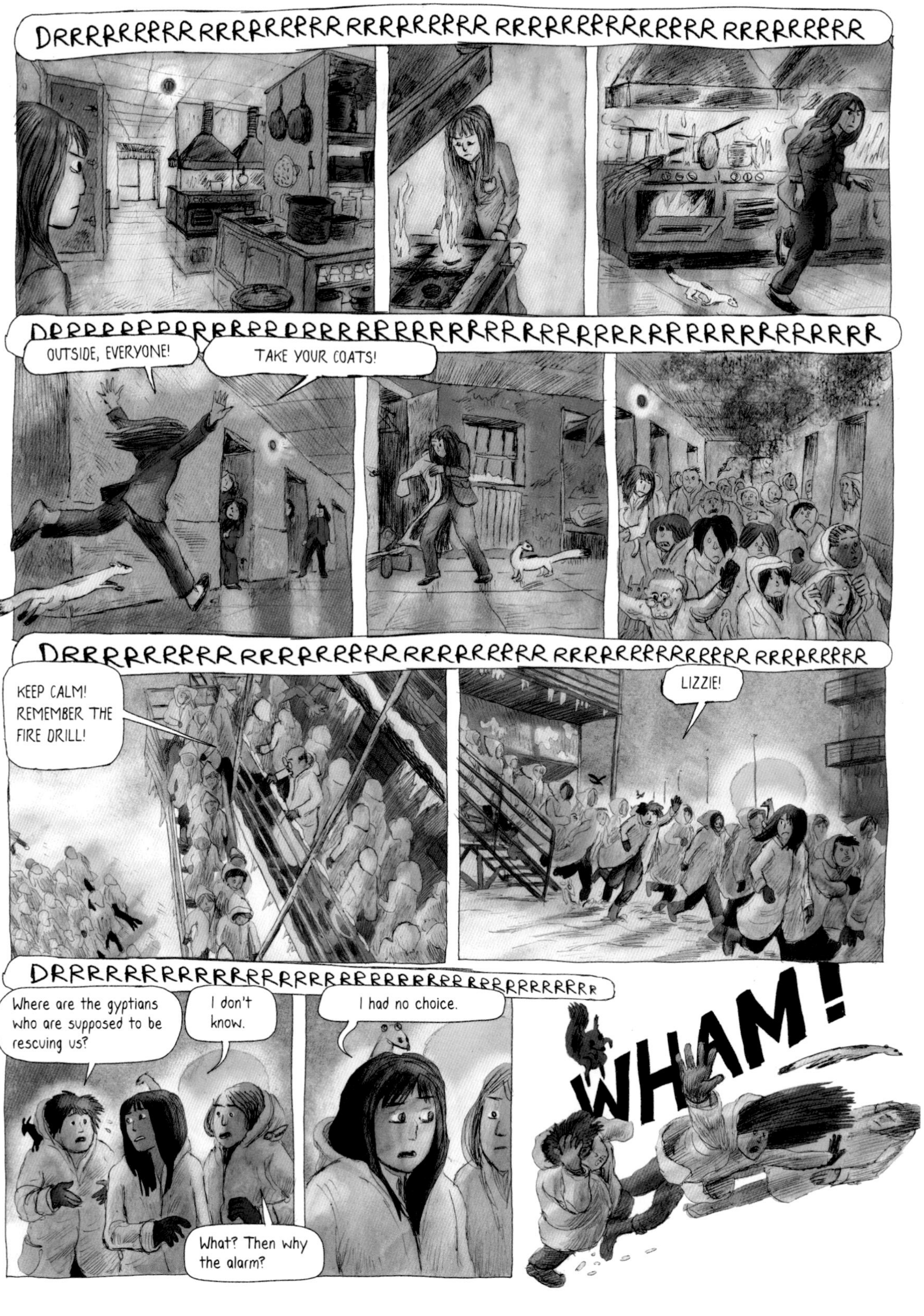
DRRRRRRRRR RRRRRRRRRR RRRRRRRRR RRRRRRRRRRRRRR RRRRRRRRR
DRRRRRRRRRRRRRRRRRRRRRRRRRRRRRRRRRRRRRRRRRRRRRRRRRRRR
OUTSIDE, EVERYONE!
TAKE YOUR COATS!
DRRRRRRRRR RRRRRRRRRR RRRRRRRRR RRRRRRRRRRRRRR RRRRRRRRR
KEEP CALM! REMEMBER THE FIRE DRILL!
LIZZIE!
DRRRRRRRRRRRRRRRRRRRRRRRRRRRRRRRRRRRRR
Where are the gyptians who are supposed to be rescuing us?
I don't know.
What? Then why the alarm?
I had no choice.
WHAM!

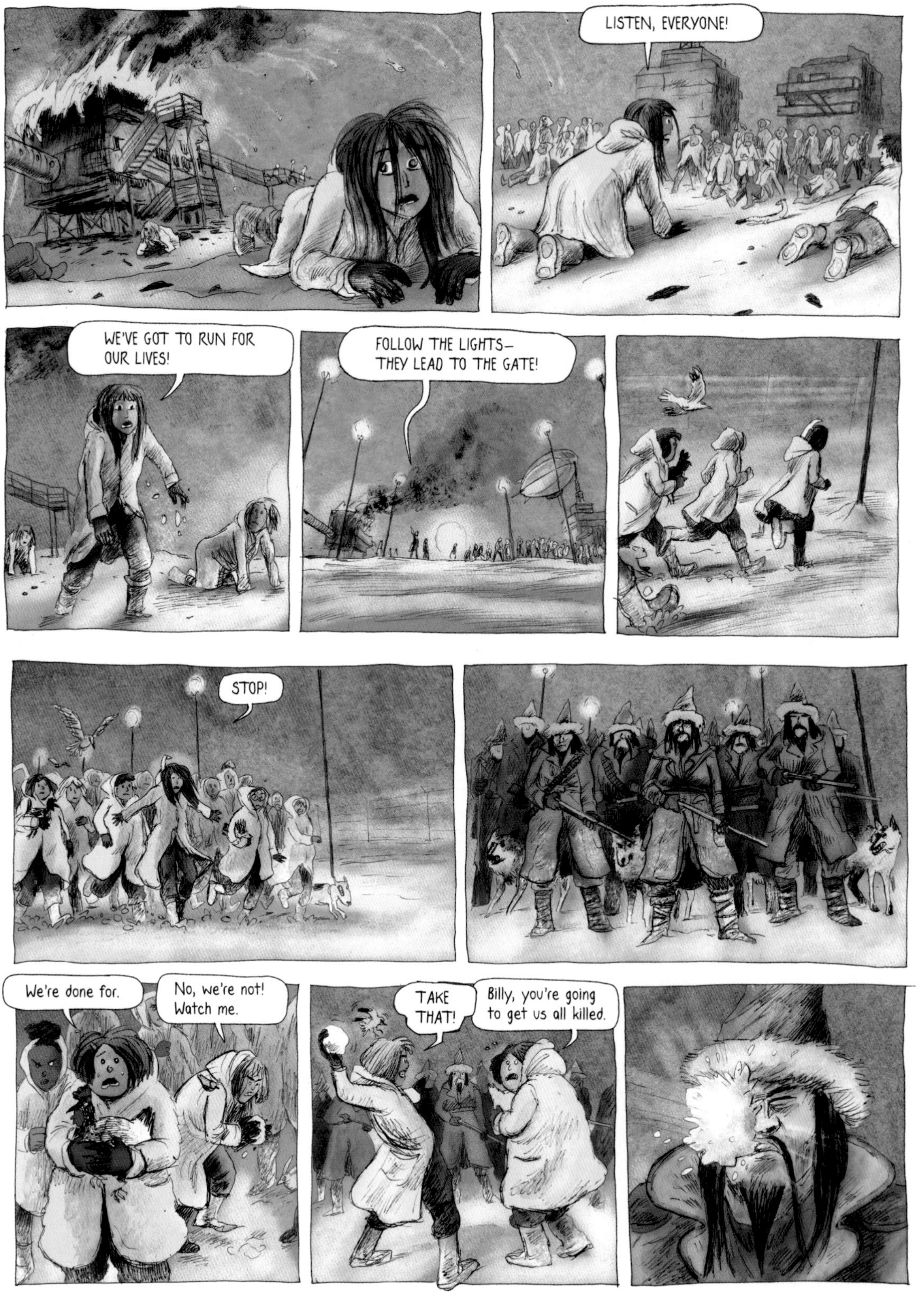
LISTEN, EVERYONE!
WE'VE GOT TO RUN FOR OUR LIVES!
FOLLOW THE LIGHTS— THEY LEAD TO THE GATE!
STOP!
We're done for.
No, we're not! Watch me.
TAKE THAT!
Billy, you're going to get us all killed.

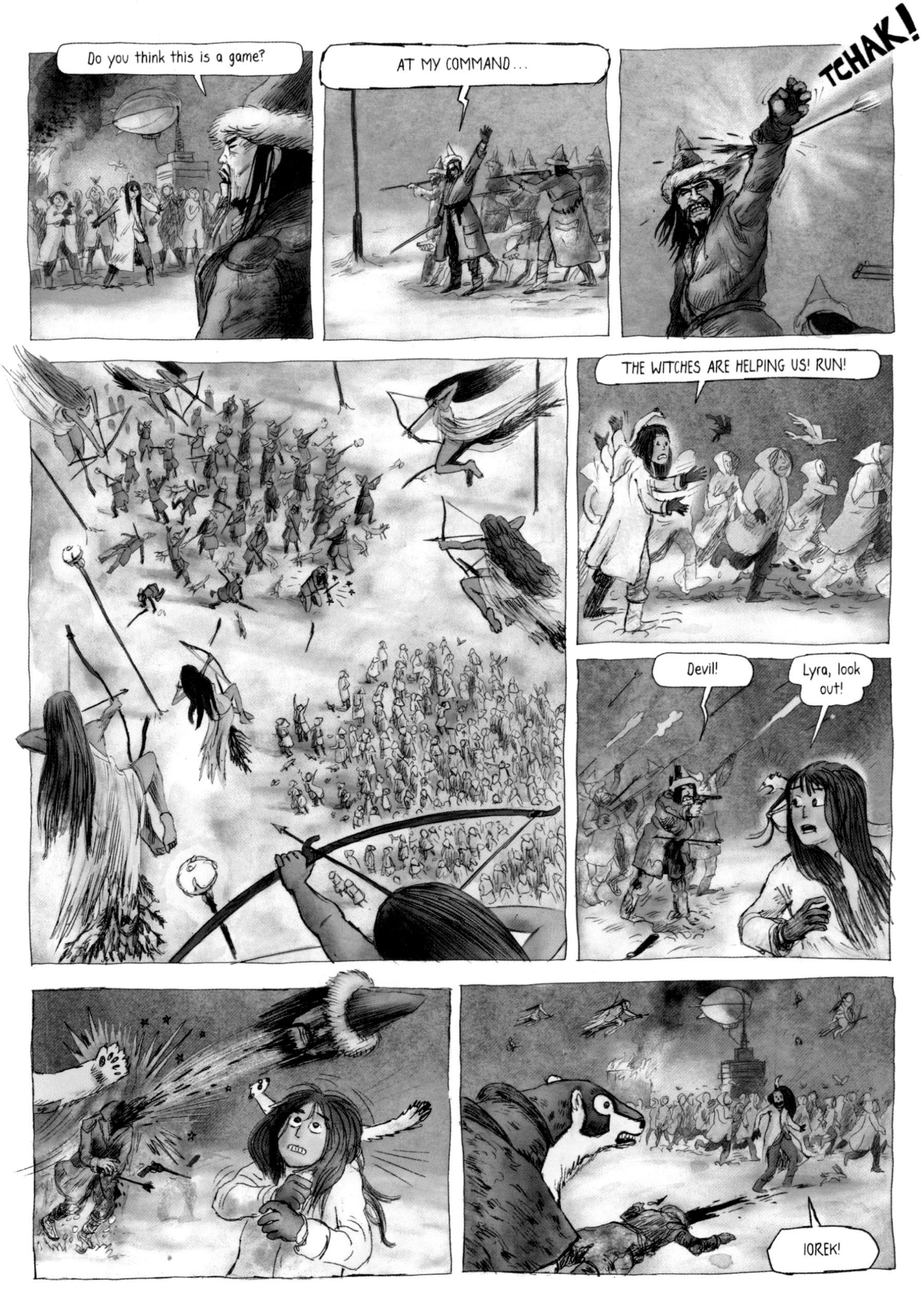
Do you think this is a game?
AT MY COMMAND...
TCHAK!
THE WITCHES ARE HELPING US! RUN!
Devil!
Lyra, look out!
IOREK!

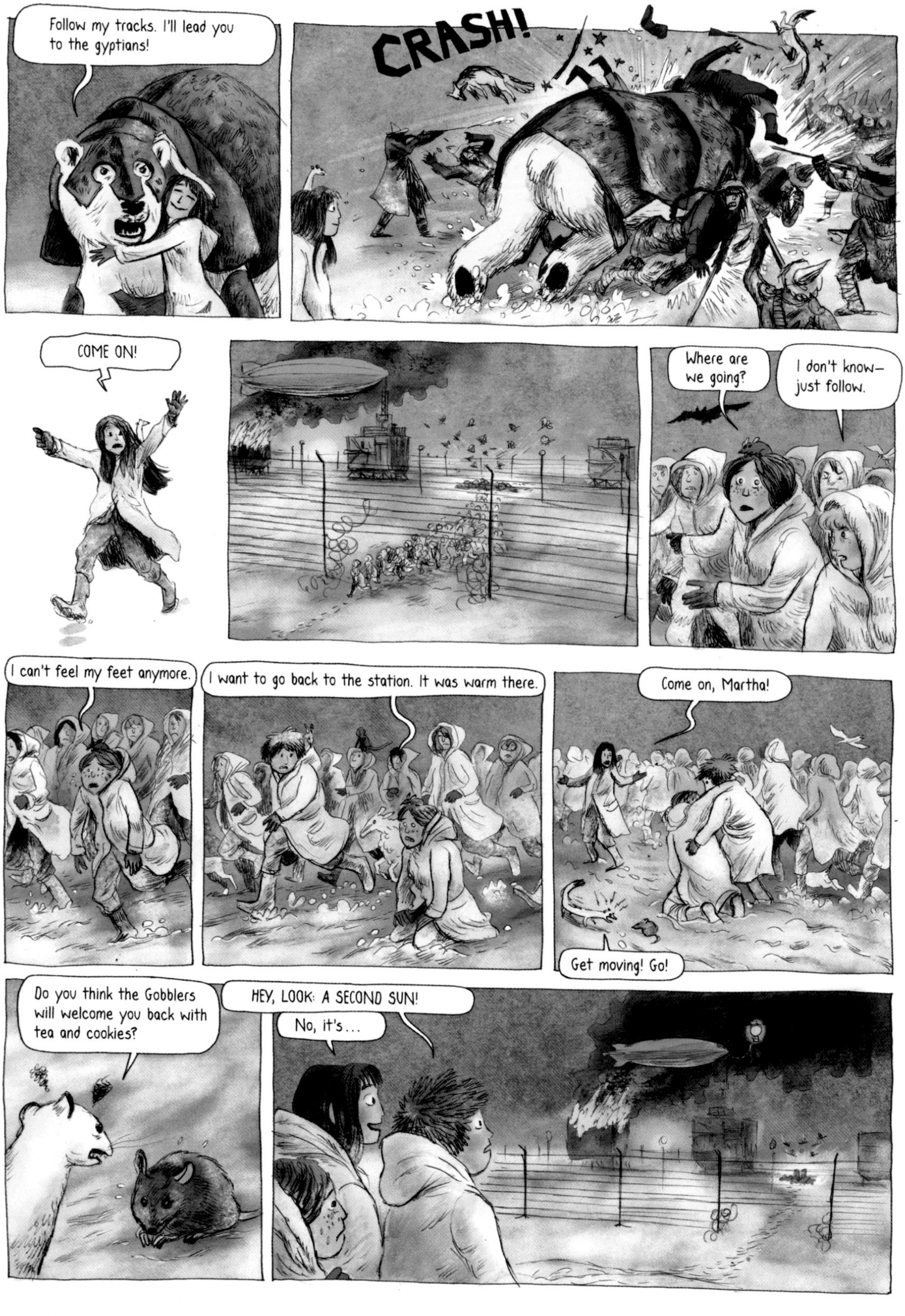

Follow my tracks. I'll lead you to the gyptians!
CRASH!
COME ON!
Where are we going?
I don't know— just follow.
I can't feel my feet anymore.
I want to go back to the station. It was warm there.
Come on, Martha!
Get moving! Go!
Do you think the Gobblers will welcome you back with tea and cookies?
HEY, LOOK: A SECOND SUN!
No, it's . . .

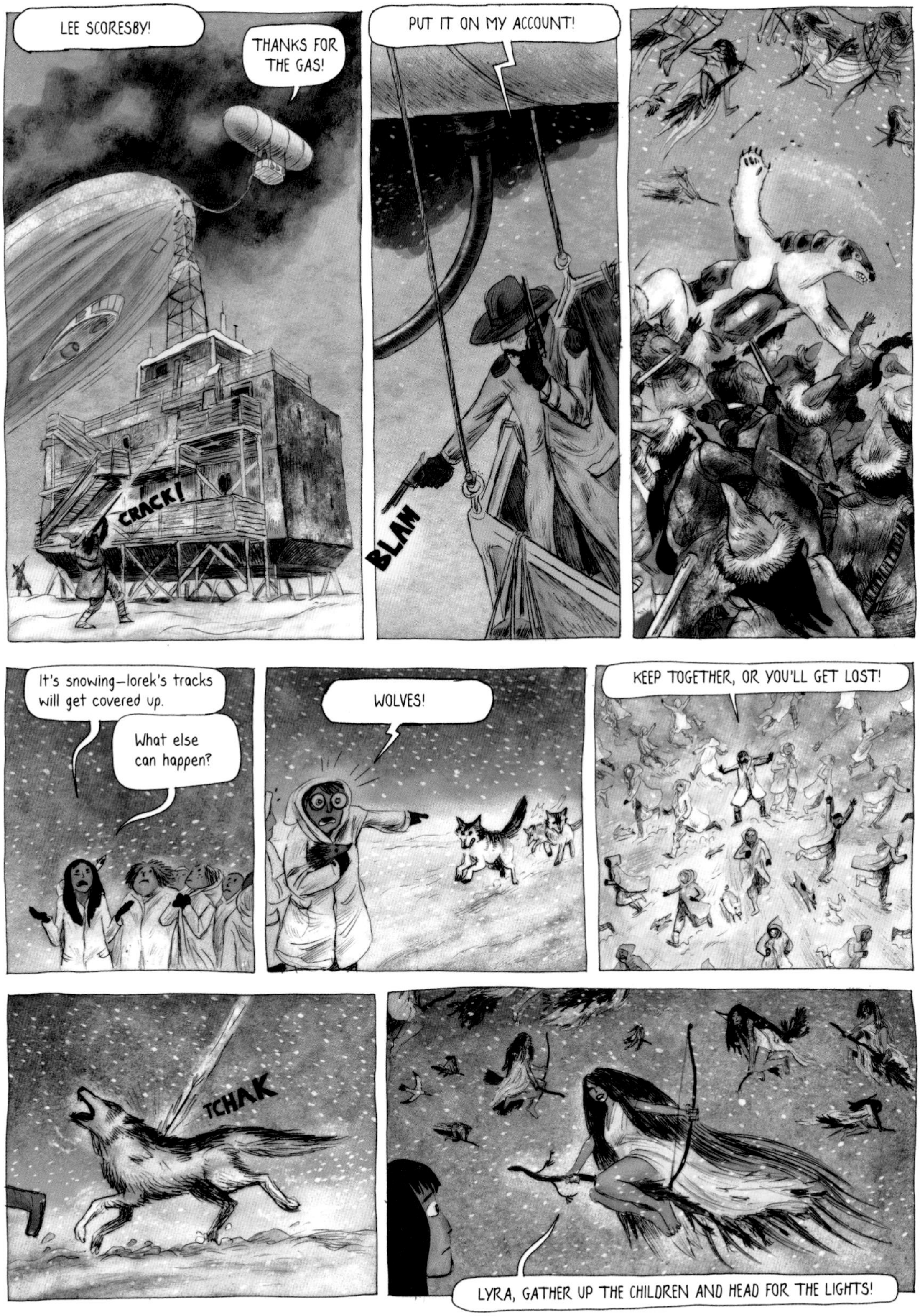
LEE SCORESBY!
THANKS FOR THE GAS!
CRACK!
PUT IT ON MY ACCOUNT!
BLAM
It's snowing—Iorek's tracks will get covered up.
What else can happen?
WOLVES!
KEEP TOGETHER, OR YOU'LL GET LOST!
TCHAK
LYRA, GATHER UP THE CHILDREN AND HEAD FOR THE LIGHTS!

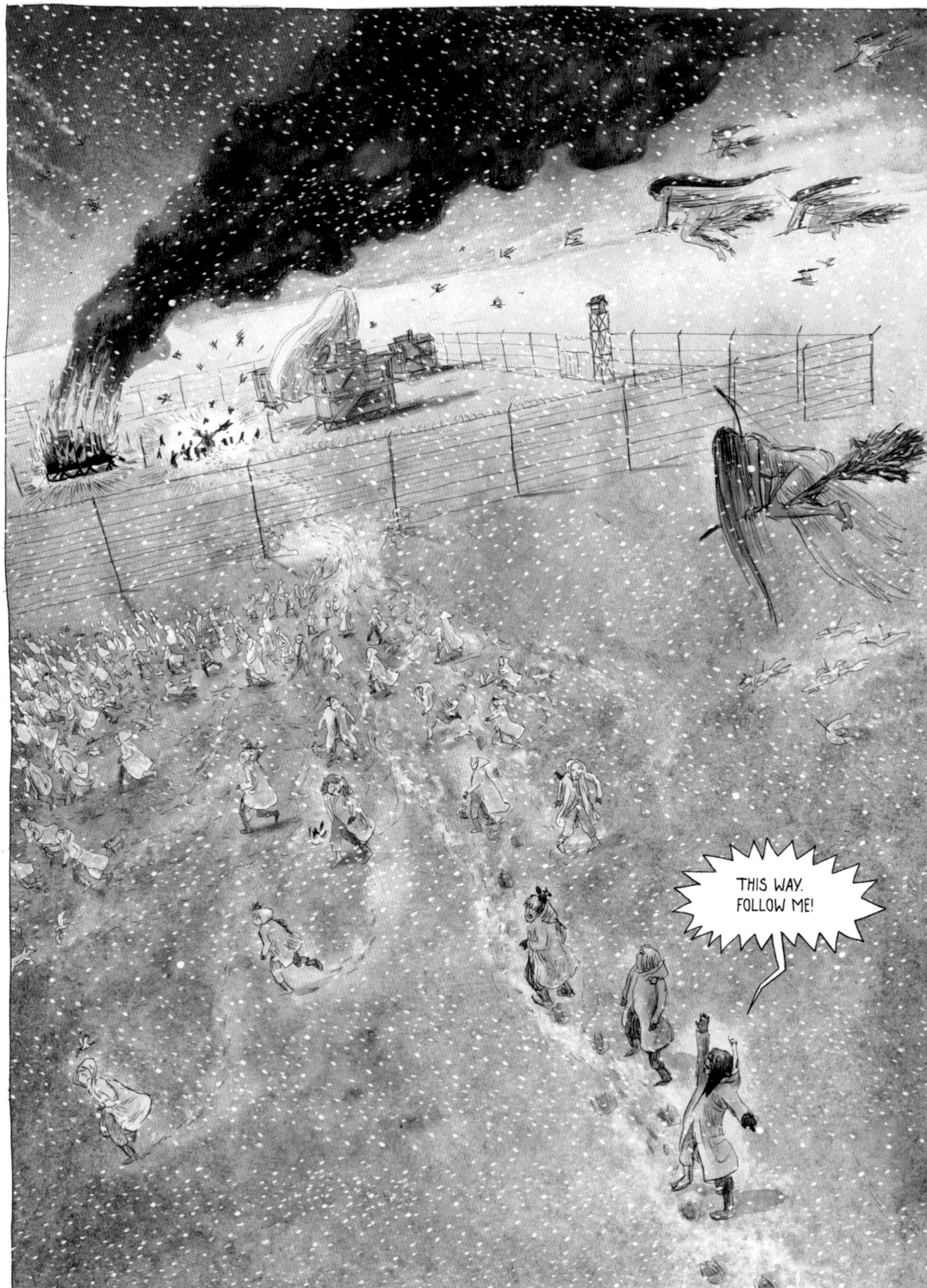
THIS WAY.
FOLLOW ME!

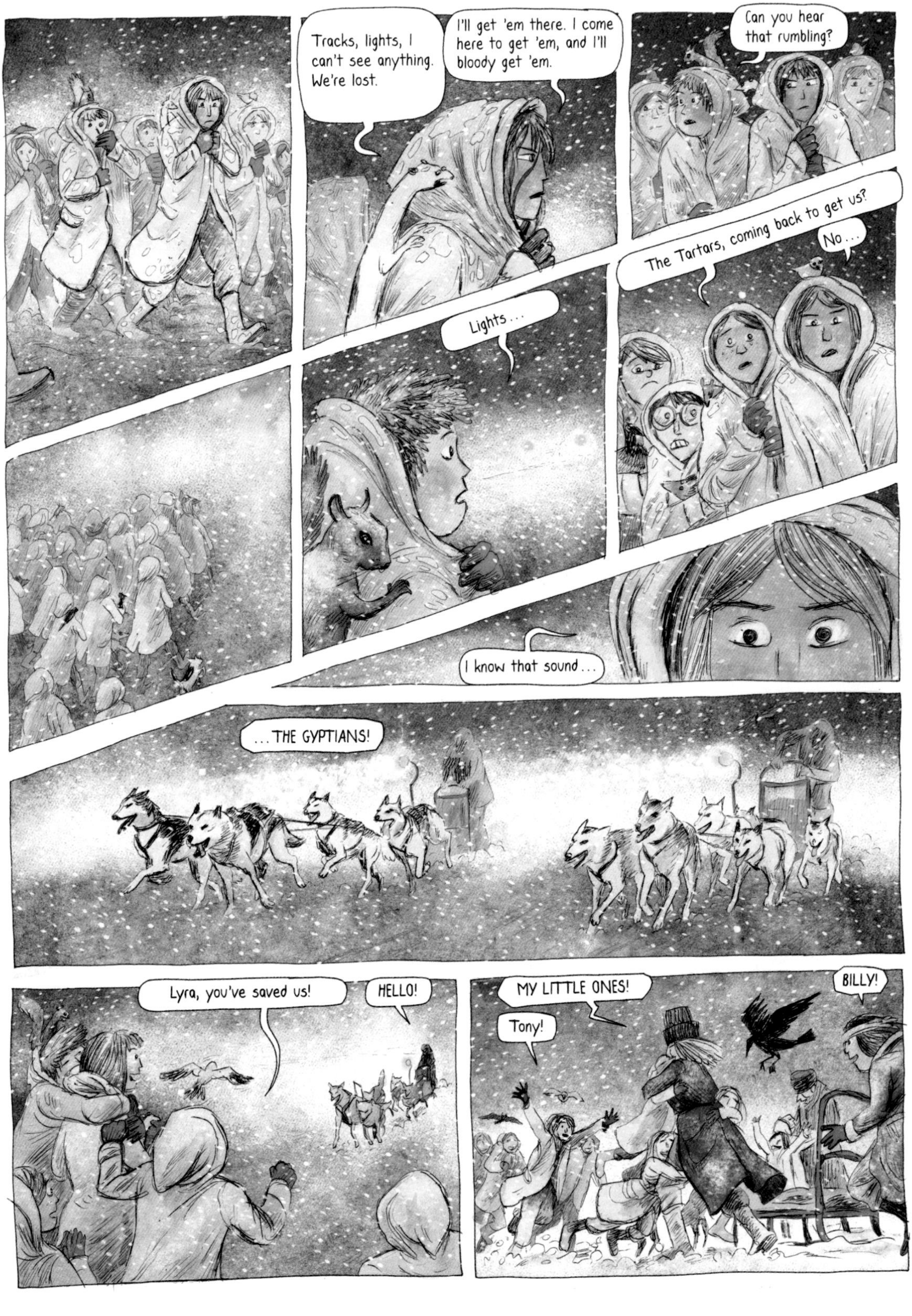

Tracks, lights, I can't see anything. We're lost.
I'll get 'em there. I come here to get 'em, and I'll bloody get 'em.
Can you hear that rumbling?
The Tartars, coming back to get us?
No ...
Lights ...
I know that sound ...
... THE GYPTIANS!
Lyra, you've saved us!
HELLO!
MY LITTLE ONES!
Tony!
BILLY!

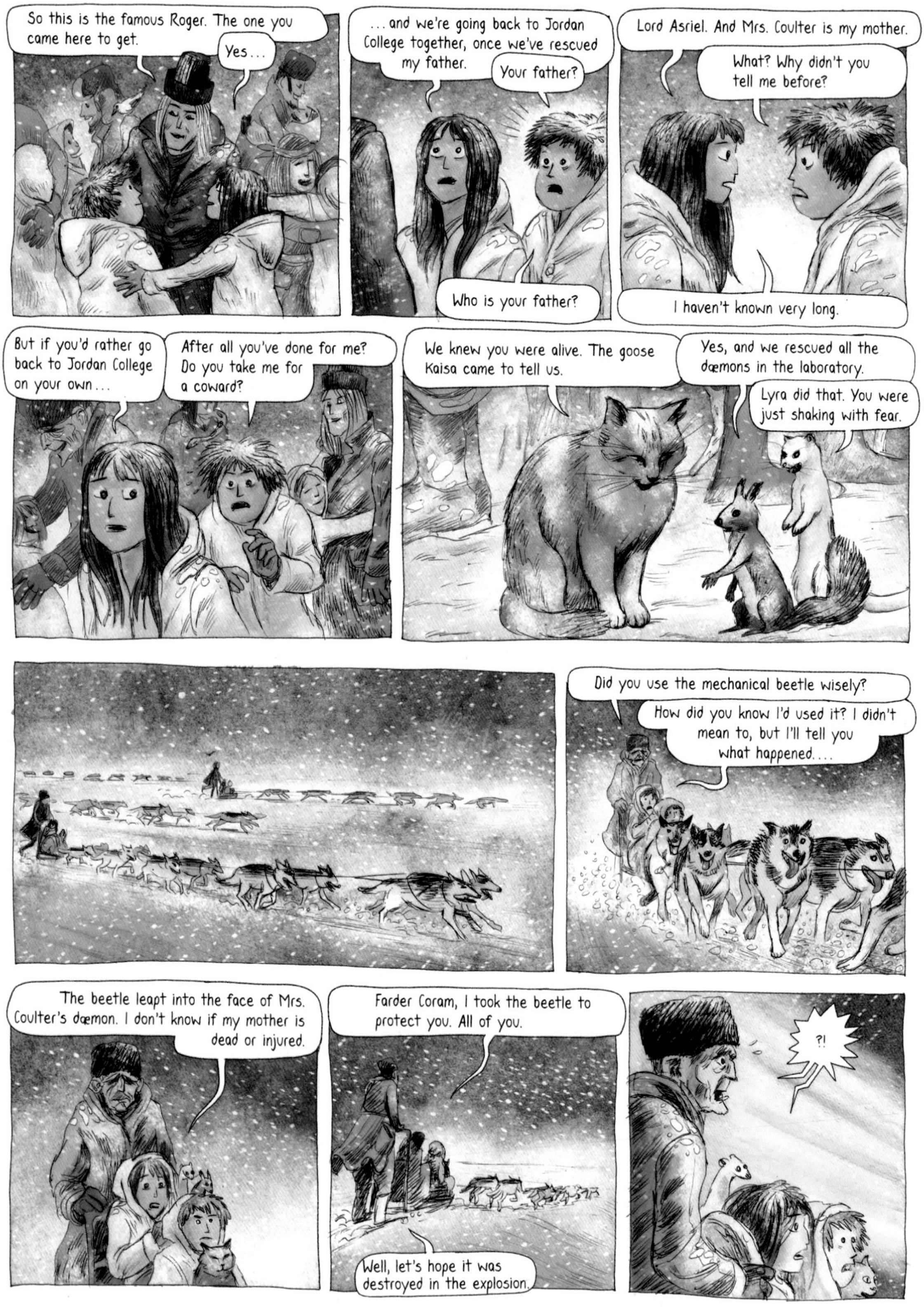
So this is the famous Roger. The one you came here to get.
Yes…
…and we're going back to Jordan College together, once we've rescued my father.
Your father?
Who is your father?
Lord Asriel. And Mrs. Coulter is my mother.
What? Why didn't you tell me before?
I haven't known very long.
But if you'd rather go back to Jordan College on your own…
After all you've done for me? Do you take me for a coward?
We knew you were alive. The goose Kaisa came to tell us.
Yes, and we rescued all the dæmons in the laboratory.
Lyra did that. You were just shaking with fear.
Did you use the mechanical beetle wisely?
How did you know I'd used it? I didn't mean to, but I'll tell you what happened….
The beetle leapt into the face of Mrs. Coulter's dæmon. I don't know if my mother is dead or injured.
Farder Coram, I took the beetle to protect you. All of you.
Well, let's hope it was destroyed in the explosion.
?!

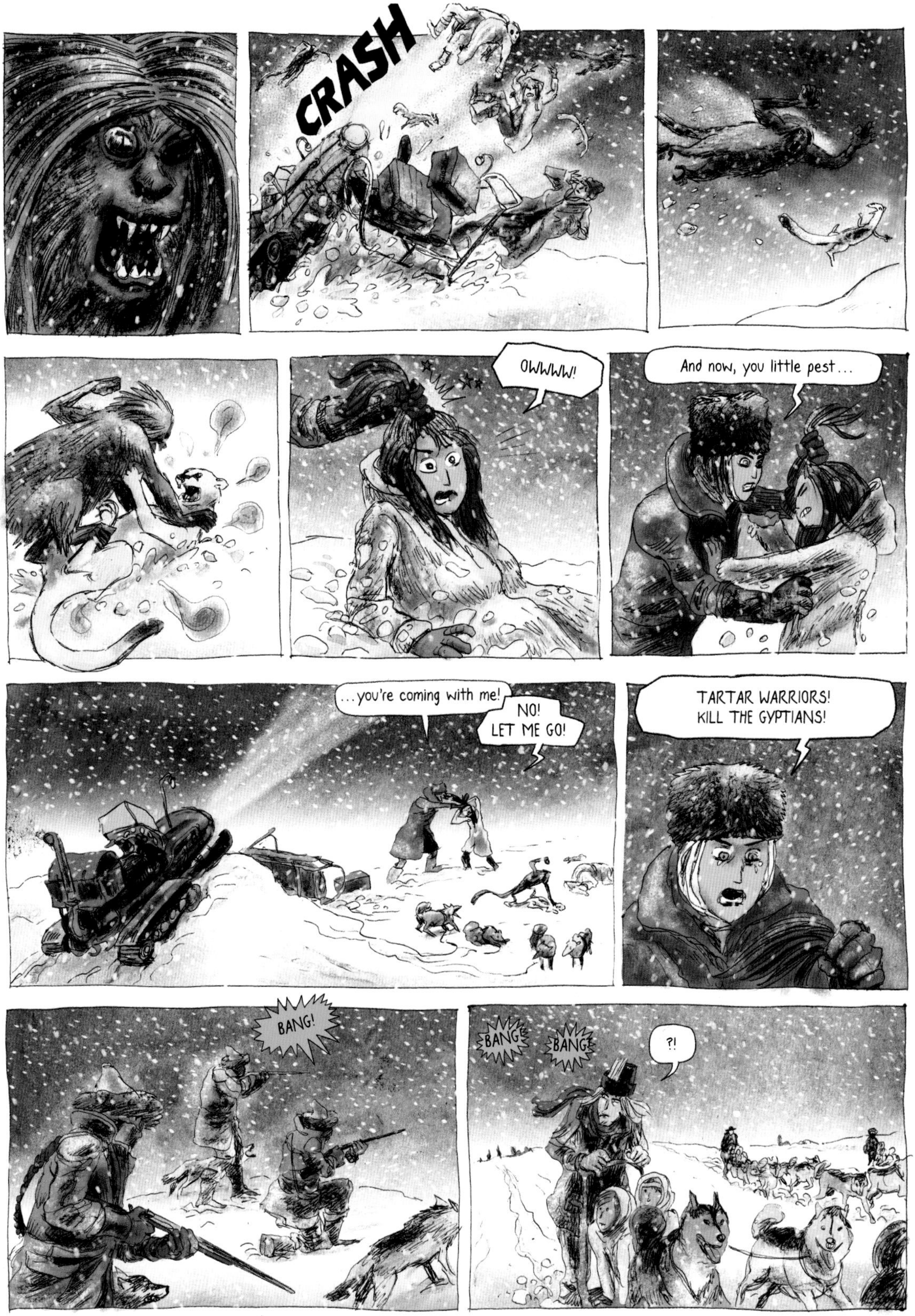
CRASH
OWWWW!
And now, you little pest...
...you're coming with me!
NO! LET ME GO!
TARTAR WARRIORS! KILL THE GYPTIANS!
BANG!
BANG!
BANG!
?!

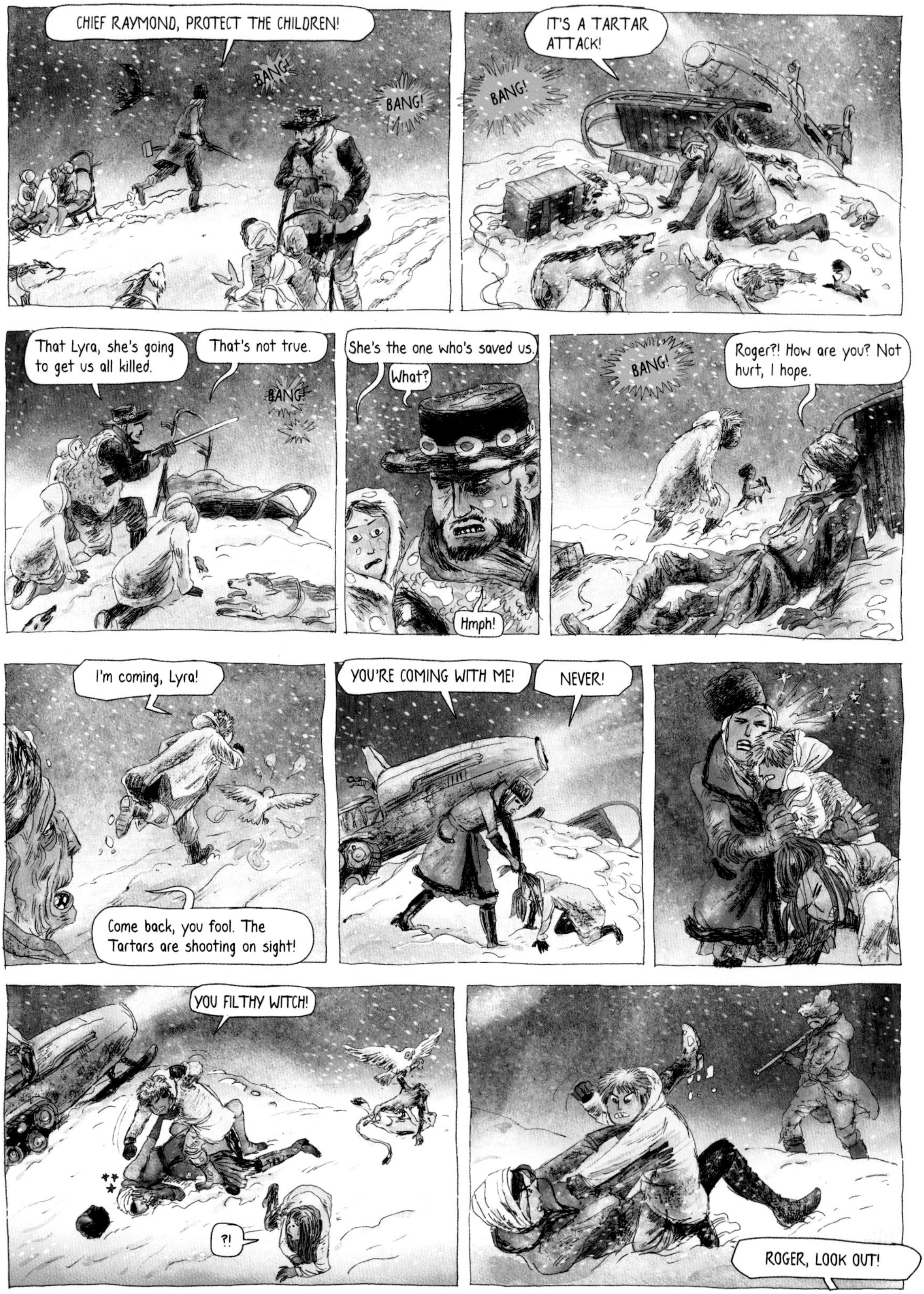
CHIEF RAYMOND, PROTECT THE CHILDREN!
BANG!
BANG!
IT'S A TARTAR ATTACK!
BANG!
That Lyra, she's going to get us all killed.
That's not true.
BANG!
She's the one who's saved us.
What?
Hmph!
BANG!
Roger?! How are you? Not hurt, I hope.
I'm coming, Lyra!
Come back, you fool. The Tartars are shooting on sight!
YOU'RE COMING WITH ME!
NEVER!
YOU FILTHY WITCH!
?!
ROGER, LOOK OUT!

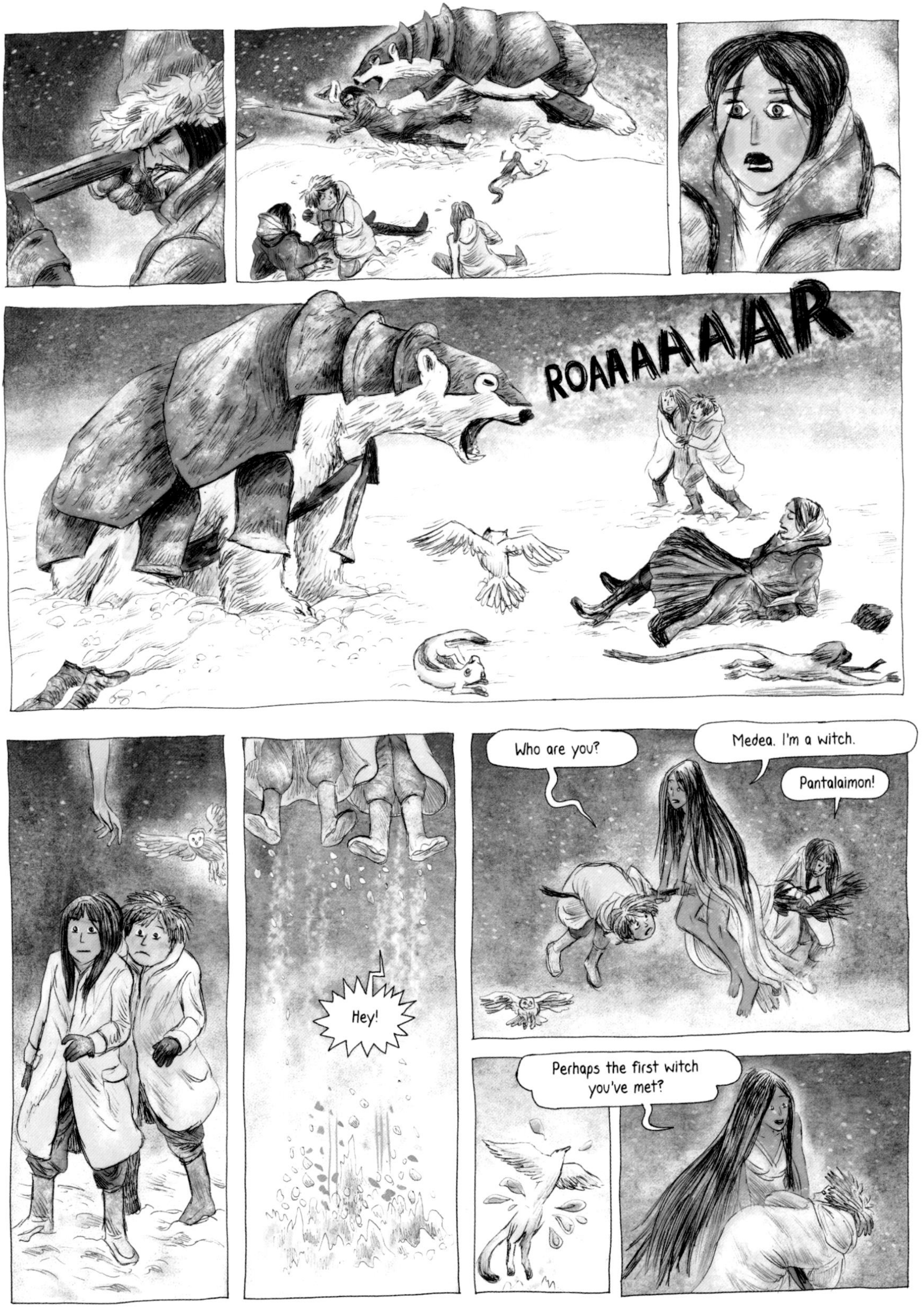
ROAAAAAAR
Hey!
Who are you?
Medea. I'm a witch.
Pantalaimon!
Perhaps the first witch you've met?

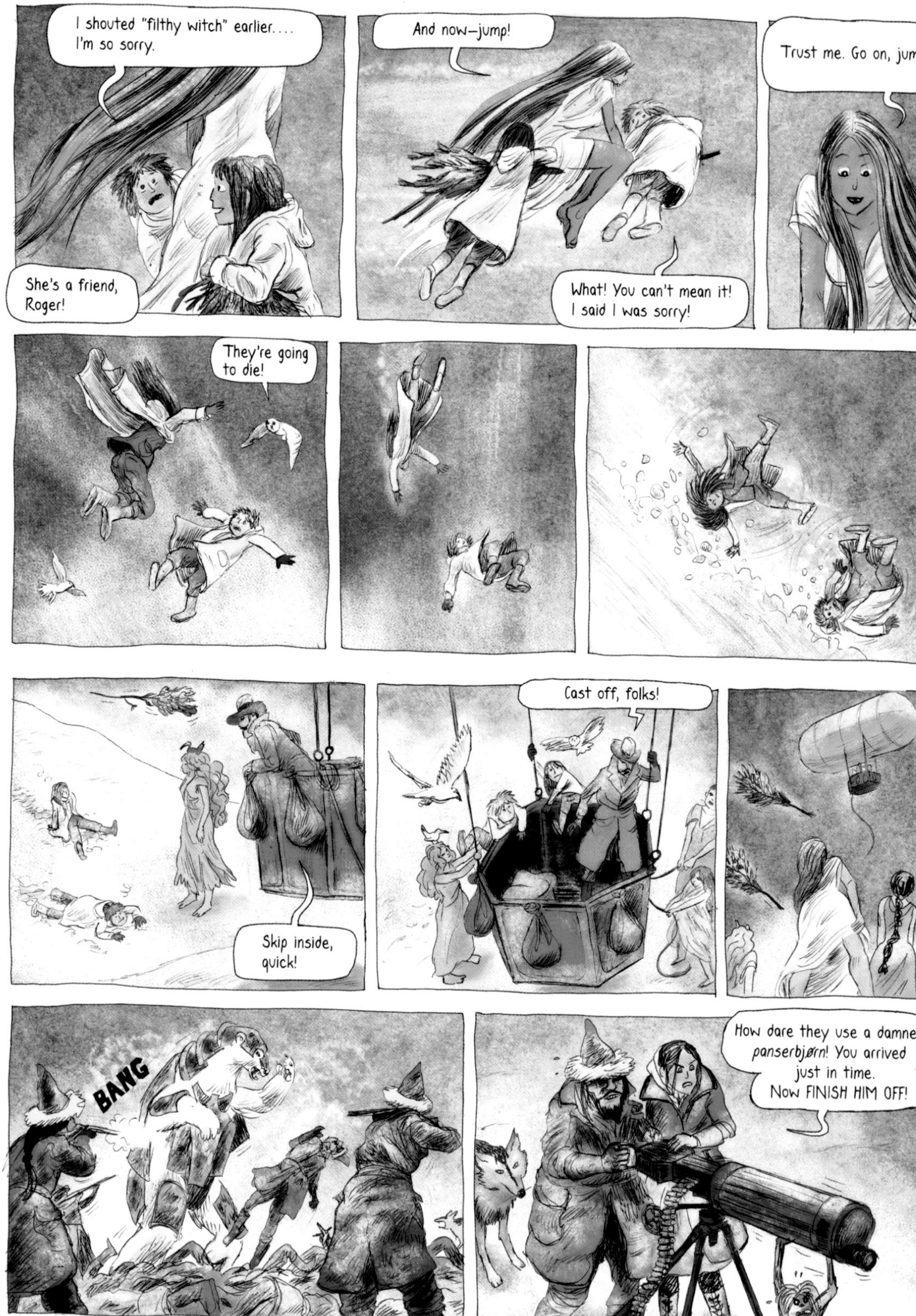
I shouted "filthy witch" earlier.... I'm so sorry.
She's a friend, Roger!
And now—jump!
What! You can't mean it! I said I was sorry!
Trust me. Go on, jump.
They're going to die!
Skip inside, quick!
Cast off, folks!
BANG
How dare they use a damned *panserbjørn*! You arrived just in time. Now FINISH HIM OFF!

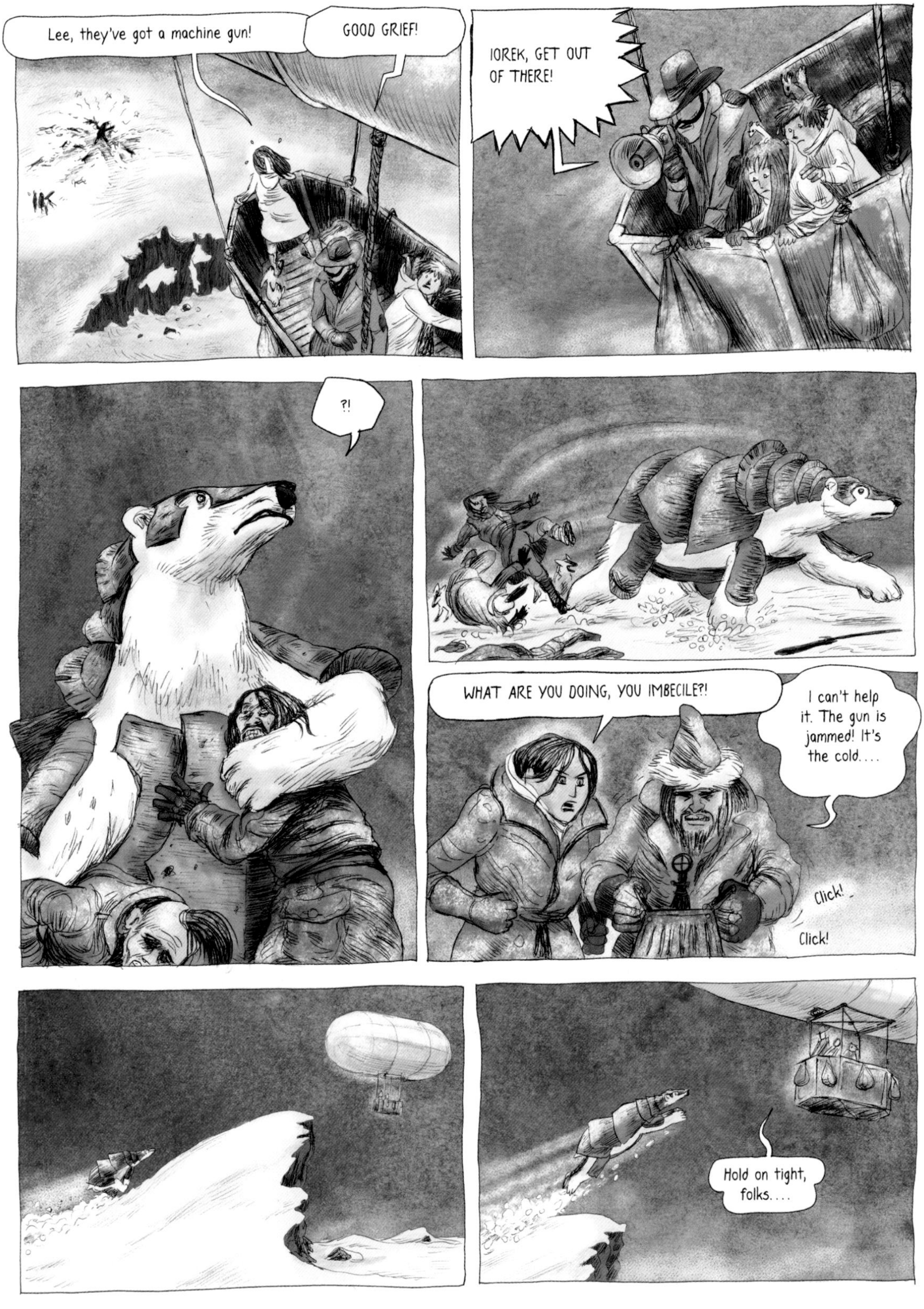
Lee, they've got a machine gun!
GOOD GRIEF!
IOREK, GET OUT OF THERE!
?!
WHAT ARE YOU DOING, YOU IMBECILE?!
I can't help it. The gun is jammed! It's the cold. . . .
Click!
Click!
Hold on tight, folks. . . .

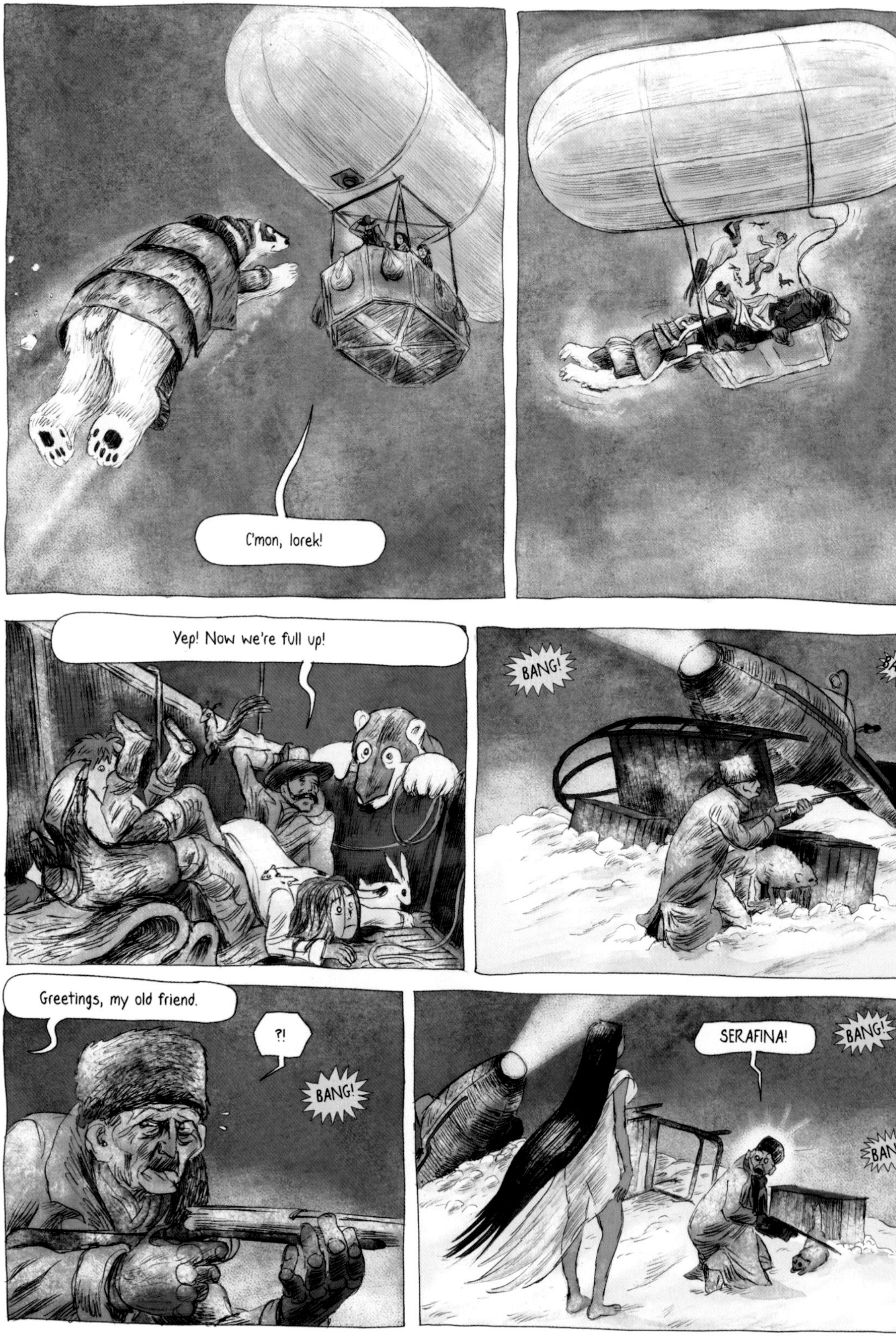

C'mon, Iorek!
Yep! Now we're full up!
BANG!
BANG!
Greetings, my old friend.
?!
BANG!
SERAFINA!
BANG!
BANG!

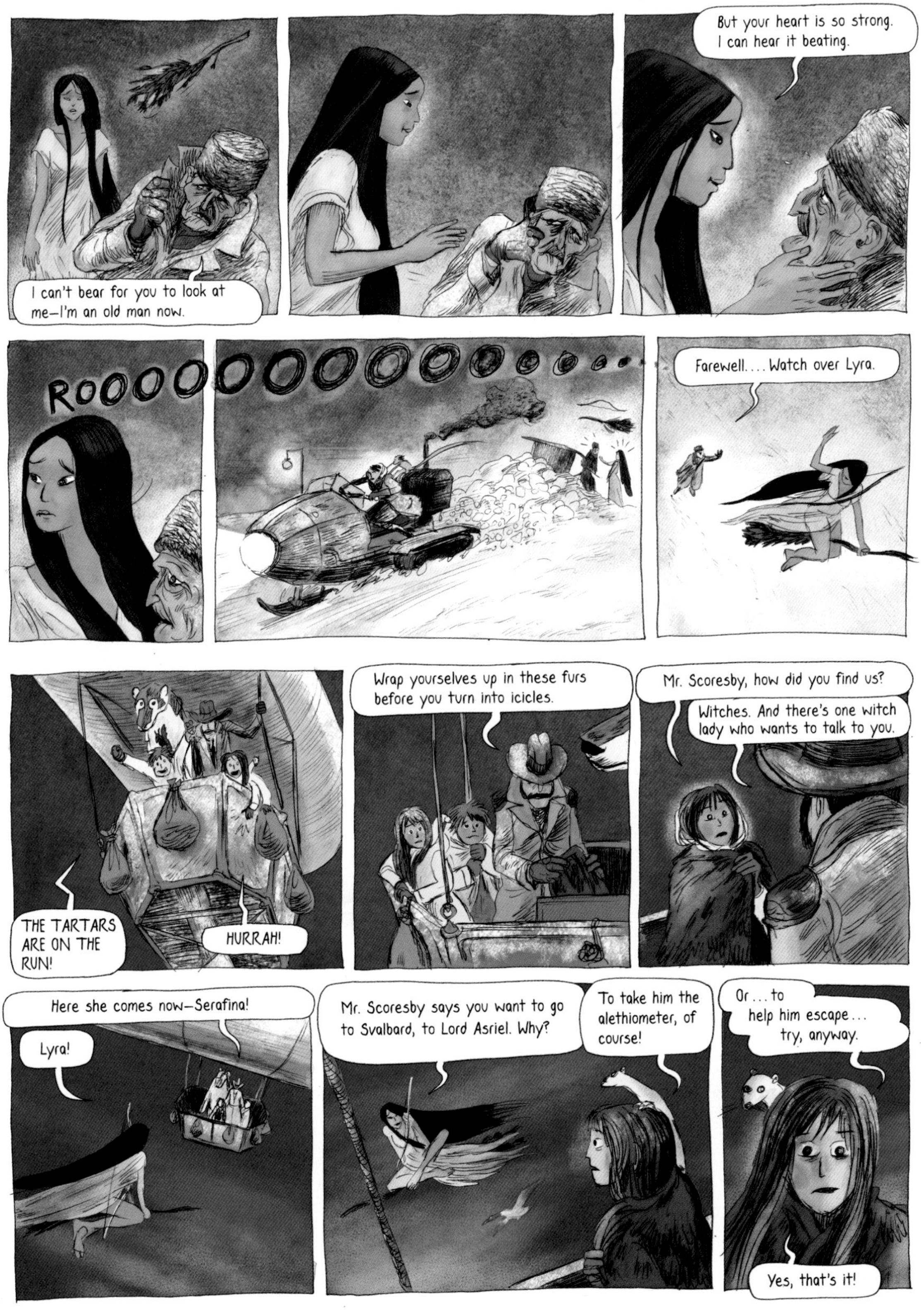
I can't bear for you to look at me—I'm an old man now.
But your heart is so strong. I can hear it beating.
ROOOOOOOOOOOOOO...
Farewell.... Watch over Lyra.
THE TARTARS ARE ON THE RUN!
HURRAH!
Wrap yourselves up in these furs before you turn into icicles.
Mr. Scoresby, how did you find us?
Witches. And there's one witch lady who wants to talk to you.
Here she comes now—Serafina!
Lyra!
Mr. Scoresby says you want to go to Svalbard, to Lord Asriel. Why?
To take him the alethiometer, of course!
Or... to help him escape... try, anyway.
Yes, that's it!

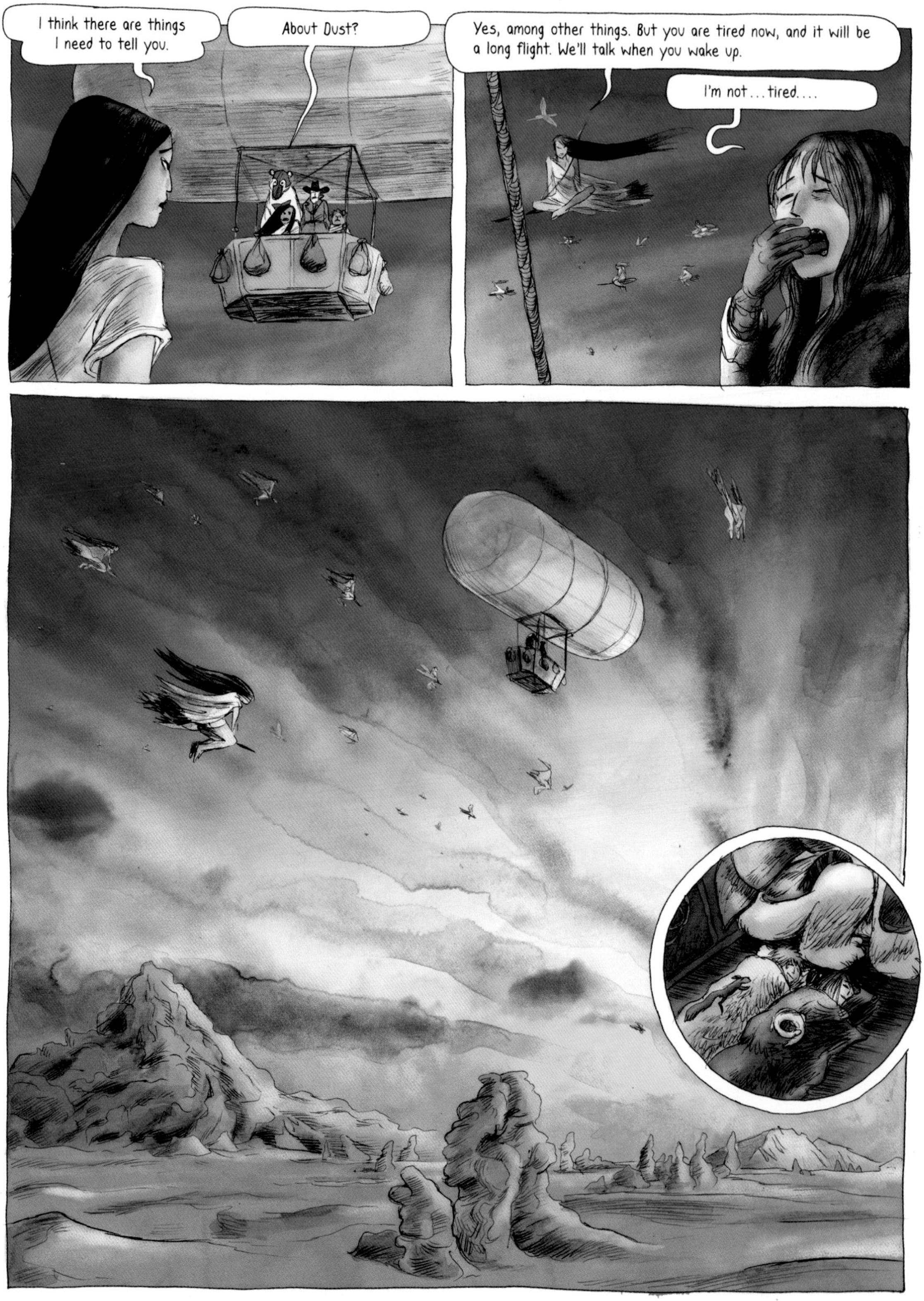
I think there are things I need to tell you.
About Dust?
Yes, among other things. But you are tired now, and it will be a long flight. We'll talk when you wake up.
I'm not . . . tired. . . .

To be continued...

0236

Lyra's journey will continue in

THE GOLDEN COMPASS

THE GRAPHIC NOVEL

VOLUME 3 coming in September 2017

HIS DARK MATERIALS

PHILIP PULLMAN
THE GOLDEN COMPASS

PHILIP PULLMAN
THE SUBTLE KNIFE

PHILIP PULLMAN
THE AMBER SPYGLASS

LYRA'S OXFORD
PHILIP PULLMAN

ONCE UPON A TIME IN THE NORTH
PHILIP PULLMAN

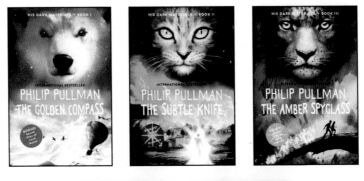

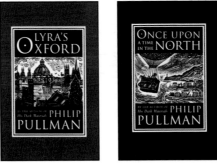

"Pullman's imagination soars. . . . A literary roller-coaster ride you won't want to miss." —*The Boston Globe*

"A literary masterpiece. . . . The most magnificent fantasy series since The Lord of the Rings." —*The Oregonian*

"Pullman is quite possibly a genius . . . using the lineaments of fantasy to tell the truth about the universal experience of growing up." —*Newsweek*